Pucking Werewolves Book 1

My
PUCKING
Mate
PREDATORS
Izzy Elliott

ISBN 978-1-964220-01-7 (Paperback)
ISBN 978-1-964220-02-4 (Hardback)
ISBN 978-1-964220-00-0 (E-Book)

Edited by Jaquelyn Vale, She Who Edits LLC
Cover Designs by Izzy Elliott (cartoons by @ArtByToniii) and Aurelia Dunbar of Mayonaka Designs
Formatting by Aurelia Dunbar of Mayonaka Designs

Printed in the United States
Published by Izzy Elliott

To YOU.

The reader who took a chance on me and my first book baby.
You'll never understand how much you mean to me.

Note from the Author

1
Leera

How did my perfect life go up in flames so quickly?

This time last year, I was in the deserts of Arizona photographing wildlife with my parents. Now, I've officially moved to the middle-of-nowhere Ohio, and my parents are . . . th-they're . . . I can feel the panic starting to set in. *Deep breath in, hold it, 5, 4, 3, 2, 1, release*—they're gone.

It was so sudden, and I'm still having a really hard time with losing them. I've never had diagnosable anxiety to the point that I needed help—that is, until everything happened. I was always a slightly anxious kid, but when you have the best parents in the world, you feel like you can handle anything, but now *they're gone.* Not like, "Hey, see you later," gone. They're gone, and they're not coming back. They went to a place that I can't follow. Not for a very long time, anyway. So now, I have to learn to navigate my life without them. Without the very people I've spent nearly every moment of my life with, for now, I've lost them, and even though I'm handling it a little better each day, it's a day I'll never forget.

Four months ago

I was sitting at the retro-red diner table in our eat-in kitchen when someone knocked on the door of our temporary rental. I wasn't expecting anyone, mostly because I don't know anyone, and Mom and Dad don't knock. I checked my smartwatch for the time and to make sure I didn't have any messages saying that they would be home soon with their arms full of groceries or something. With no warning of their arrival, I slowly rose and made my way to the old, white door. I stood on my tiptoes to check the peephole, spotting a somber-looking man in a uniform. "Who are you?" I hollered through the door. I don't know this guy; there is no way I am opening this door.

"Officer Bentley, ma'am, with the Phoenix Police Department. Are you Leera? Leera Adams?" he replied, holding his badge up to the peephole for me to see. Satisfied, I slowly opened the door, and with my arms crossed, I stepped back to try to keep a safe distance.

"Um, yes, what exactly can I do for you?" I asked my dirty, used-to-be-white shoes, hoping we could get whatever this is done quickly.

"May I come in? I need to speak with you, and I think it would be best if we could have a seat." He slowly stepped over the threshold, hands where I could see them. He cautiously raised his right hand, directing me back toward the old, red table I was just seated at. I lowered myself back onto my chair and pushed my homework away.

My heart felt like an angry woodpecker was trying to break

out of my chest. My hands were trembling and freezing cold, but somehow I was sweating. *What in the world is going on?*

I hadn't had a lot of interaction with law enforcement or people in general. I'd been homeschooled my whole life. My mom, dad, and I traveled the world, mostly the US, for their jobs. Mom was a photographer, and Dad was a journalist; together, they were one of the most sought-after photojournalist teams in the business. They could always get the perfect shot that no one else was able to capture. They found the animals and plant life that expertly evaded everyone else's lenses. A few times, they even rediscovered something that was believed to be extinct!

So, I may not have had the typical childhood, but I loved every minute of it. I never really felt envious of other kids' experiences because I was always just so happy. Sure, I wondered what a normal life would look like, but at the end of the day, I couldn't give up these amazing experiences. I had the absolute best parents in the world while exploring the *literal* world. Anyone who can complain about something so amazing is beyond me.

The officer cleared his throat. I was so lost in my head that I forgot he was here. I forgot that something seemed to be wrong. How could I forget that, even for a moment? I sighed and slowly looked up, still not quite making eye contact. "Can you please tell me what's going on? You're kind of freaking me out."

He sighed, twisting his hands in his lap. He stood and paced around the room for a moment before he took a deep breath and looked at me with the saddest, grey-blue eyes I'd ever seen. *Oh no, something's wrong. Something is very wrong. Where's Mom and Dad? Shouldn't they be here for whatever he's about to say?*

"Ma'am, do you have any family you can call that you can stay with for a little while?" he asked softly. His mousy-brown hair was a mess, like he'd been running his hands through it.

"No, my mom and dad went out on a photoshoot, and I was finishing up my homework. They'll be home any minute. Maybe we should wait for them. Here, let me call them and see where they are. I'll let them know you're here and that they need to come home." I knew I was rambling, but I couldn't stop, and the phone just kept ringing and ringing.

The officer slowly reached for my phone and set it face down on the table. He kneeled down in front of me and grabbed my small, trembling hands covered in a thin layer of cold sweat, in his. With his large, rough hands wrapped around mine, he stared at the floor for a moment before looking me in the eyes as he said, "I'm sorry, Leera, can you slow down and focus for me?" I barely nodded, but he saw the slight motion. "Leera, your parents can't answer the phone."

That's ridiculous; my parents always answered the phone. They have never, in the history of me calling them, not answered the phone. *What was going on? Were they okay?*

"Leera, look at me. Your parents can't answer the phone. There was a car accident on the—"

"Oh my gosh, they've been in an accident?! Are they okay? Are they in the hospital? Can you take me to them?" I was rambling again, but again, I couldn't stop. Stopping meant he could keep talking and tell me something I didn't want to hear. The shaking and the angry bird in my chest were getting worse. They were now joined by a heavy weight pressing down on me, making it hard for me to take a deep breath.

The officer squeezed my hands that he was still holding and

waited for me to refocus on him. In that moment, it felt like someone dropped a lead weight in my stomach, and my eyes were burning with tears that hadn't fallen yet. "Please tell me they're okay and you're here to take me to them," I whispered just loud enough for him to hear me.

"I'm so sorry, but your parents didn't survive the accident. They were already gone when we found the car. Do you have anyone you can call?"

No one. I had no one. It was always just the three of us. Neither of them had any living family. We never needed anyone else. We were the Three Musketeers. We did everything together—just the three of us. I was all alone. Truly and completely alone. *What am I going to do?*

The dam of tears was released before I could even feel it coming. Twin saltwater streams cascaded down my face, but no sound came out. I slowly shook my head at the officer and looked around the rental. *Is this really happening?*

"What do I do?" I whispered with a sniffle, "This is a short-term rental for their current job, before we moved on to the next one. Where are they? Can I see them? Maybe it's not them. They were the nicest people ever; maybe they just let someone borrow their car. What do I do? Mom is supposed to take me shopping for my dorm room tomorrow. What do I do?"

My breaths were coming faster and faster while the tears held a steady pace down my cheeks, but other than my running thoughts, no sounds came out. This can't be real. I have to be dreaming. I've fallen asleep while working on my homework, and Mom and Dad will wake me up any minute so that we can check my work and cook dinner together. It's Tuesday, and we always have tacos together because it's Taco Tuesday.

Just then, a small knock sounded on the door. I lurched towards the door so fast that I almost ran right into the kitchen counter. I knew they had to be okay; I knew they weren't gone, but wait—I came to a crashing halt, just steps from the door—*Mom and Dad don't knock . . .*

Once again, I lifted myself onto my toes to check the peephole. This time there was a small woman with a folder in her arms. Officer Bentley reached around me to open the door and gave the woman a sad smile. "Hi Shelia, this is Leera," he stopped talking, and they seemed to exchange a silent conversation where she was asking him questions with her eyebrows, and he gave her a short, clipped nod.

I was taken aback by whatever secret, silent conversation they had, knowing that what was said could not be good news, and hopefully not worse news, for that matter. I froze, realizing that if it were true, if my parents were really gone, my life would be completely turned upside down. I stared blankly at the professionally dressed woman standing in my doorway, and I'd started to become overly anxious. To avoid having a complete breakdown in front of two strangers, I focused on her outfit. I couldn't help but notice that her business suit matched the color of her hair—salt and pepper.

Getting knocked back into reality, a reality I really did not want to face. The woman took both my hands in hers and walked me further into the rental toward the uncomfortable black leather couch. I've always hated this couch. We were in Arizona. It was always hot, and your legs stuck to it and got all sweaty. It wasn't a couch for snuggling together to watch a movie. It was the stuffy couch of someone who cared more about how something looked than its comfort and usefulness. I'd been so excited to move on to the next job, just to get away from that couch.

Over the next hour, we discussed what they found and what that meant for me. Since I had nobody I could call, I got a case worker, even though I would turn eighteen in a couple weeks. Apparently, the case worker was supposed to help me make sure my "affairs were in order" before I went off to college in August. They advised that it was in my best interest to not see the state of my parents and that they'd make sure I got all their belongings as soon as possible. Then, after what felt like a lifetime, they both gave me their phone numbers in case I needed anything, made sure I was okay to be alone, and then left.

I slowly closed the door, leaning my whole body against it as I did, and locked it. I turned around, leaned my back onto the door, slowly slid down, wrapped my arms around my legs, and sobbed uncontrollably. The tears were finally accompanied by what I can only describe as fresh waves of hell. My body felt like it was being ripped apart from the inside out, while the outside was still cold and clammy. I rocked back and forth, willing the pain away, begging Mom and Dad to please just walk through the door. *How could a broken heart hurt worse than any physical wound I'd ever endured? How could a heart break so thoroughly and keep beating?*

Hours later, they hadn't come home. I awoke on the floor in front of the door. I don't know if I passed out from lack of oxygen or if I cried myself to sleep. Tapping my watch awake, I noticed that it was just before midnight. After pulling myself out of the heap I was lying in, I wrapped my arms back around my legs and just stared around the room for a minute. My watch beeped, letting me know I missed my vitamin reminder. Mom and Dad took vitamins very seriously. A healthy life is a happy life, and all that. *A lot of good that did them.* I climbed to my feet but had to lean on the door for support for a moment as my legs had that awful tingling feeling from being asleep. It hurt and tickled and was so uncomfortable, but they finally subsided enough for me to make it to the kitchen cabinet where we kept all our vitamins.

Swallowing them down with a glass of tap water, I took a moment to be thankful that my vitamins were one less thing I had to worry about.

After I had decided to head to college in the fall, Dad had immediately bought all my necessities for my first six months of school. He was the planner of the family. Mom was very whim-sical where he needed order. They were a perfectly balanced pair. Mom and Dad always told me I was the best of both of them and I had to agree, I felt like I had a happy-whimsy-ordered balance.

As my mind quieted, I found myself with my head tilted back and just staring at the ceiling. *What was I going to do without them?*

Present

A small sob chokes out of me, knocking me back to reality. Shaking my head, I look around the small, drab space I will be sharing with a relative stranger for at least the next six months. Mom would have so many ideas for our little room, and they would have all been perfect.

Channeling my inner whimsy, I make a list of things to brighten the space and make it feel more like home. Make it feel more like my mom was actually able to take me shopping that day. I vow to choose at least one thing that I find hideous, that dad would have simply shaken his head at, that she would have loved.

Happy with my list, I set to unpacking. Since I was used to moving around all the time, I didn't have much to unpack. I ordered one of those POD storage unit things for my mom and dad's stuff that I couldn't part with. That way, when I finish school and settle down, I can have it delivered to me. Setting a picture of the three of us on my desk, I touch their faces and smile. "I love you guys. I wish you could be here. I hope I can do this without you."

I allow myself one more tear before promising to focus on happiness. The therapist I had in Arizona was so sweet and gave me so many tools to help manage my grief and anxiety. I would have been truly lost without her. Referring me to her was the only helpful thing my worthless caseworker did.

After just an hour of unpacking my little box of stuff, my watch beeps again, reminding me to take my vitamins.

Content with my progress, I curl up in bed and browse Mom and Dad's Instagram account. Seeing their work brings me peace. Remembering my old life hurts a lot more some days than others, but I know they would want me to be happy, so I'm really trying. I'm taking this amazing opportunity given to me, and I'm going to start this new life with happiness and good intentions.

My roommate is supposed to be here tomorrow, and I want to be well rested so we can get off on the right foot. We've been talking all summer, and we've hit it off really well, but you never know what will happen in real life.

I mean, I've never had a real friend before, outside of my parents. Sure, I might have made quick friends with the guides or tribes when we were on assignment, but since I've never gone to school and their work consisted of nature and wildlife photography all over the world, I really never settled down or socialized. I'm worried I'll be awkward and strange, but I hope we can be friends.

Maybe once I'm good and settled, I can even meet someone. Obviously, never having friends, I never had anyone to be interested in. That's another thing my parents did well. They showed me that when you love and choose the right person to spend your life with, it's really not that far off from the movies. They would dance in the kitchen at night after cleaning up from dinner, constantly holding hands and kissing each other in public, and my dad was always buying her flowers or little tokens of love just because. I don't expect to find "the one" necessarily, but maybe I could date a few people and test the waters. Maybe I could just get my first kiss.

With my mind busy and my body tired, having successfully completed the first day of my new life, I finally put my phone on the charger and call it a night.

2
ROMAN

I'm not sure what I would do without hockey.

I'd be lying if I said that I wasn't intrigued when hockey first came about a hundred years ago, give or take. At the time, I never had the chance to really try it out to see if it was a right fit for me—not right away at least.

Being the commander of a relatively out-of-shape army came with a heavy workload. It wasn't until I got them all straightened out and in working order before I could explore more relaxed activities. I never really wanted anything to do with our armies, but my father was born without status and was never able to acquire one for himself. Apparently, even being best friends with the king's advisor wasn't enough for him to get his way; that is, until he had me. He raised me to be everything he wasn't. He loathed his parents for settling for normalcy when he was destined for greatness, or so he says. He spent my life molding me into exactly what the king needed, which was a warrior. Not just any warrior, but a leader. His military was solid if needed for defensive purposes, but that was all. It took hundreds of years, but I trained and built them into an elite machine that can conquer, defend, and protect.

Benny and I started learning and practicing hockey together about thirty years ago. The nineties were an amazing time for the NHL. Wayne Gretzky, need I say more? As for Benny and me, we don't do anything with less than perfection, so we spent a couple decades honing our skills to be the best before we decided to go pro. The rest of my closest men saw us enjoying ourselves and joined in a while later.

It has always amazed me that humans just believe that there are other humans with basically the same DNA as each other that are just that much bigger, stronger, faster, and tougher. Pretty much all professional sports are played by a supernatural being, or their less-blood offspring. While most paranormal creatures' mate and marry within their species, sometimes fate has other plans. Since we're immortal, it's nice to have something to do to pass the time now. The world was so much more boring before organized sports.

Anyway, Benny and I chose hockey. We love the cold, the competition, and getting to beat the shit out of other wolves. Thanks to our supernatural healing abilities, it looks a lot worse than it really is, and we're usually as right as rain after about an hour or so. Since the US hasn't adopted rugby yet, this is as good as it gets.

I'd wanted to start a new hockey team in a more rural setting but close enough to big cities that we have everything we need. After digging around and checking out our options, we set up in Mogadore, Ohio. It's less than a handful of hours from my pack, with plenty of close city access, plenty of wooded areas, and lots of corn fields. We're the Mogadore Predators.

Another thing humans don't know is that when a supernatural being wants to get involved in a sports team, they can contact an existing team, or if they have enough men and money, they can start their own. We choose someone else to be the team owner, sometimes even letting humans take the reins on the business side of things. Our publicized team owner is a half-werewolf kid named Kit. He's about two hundred and fifty years old, he's good at business, and the guys love him. I say publicized because he's fifty percent owner. I own the rest of the team, but I don't want the attention or notoriety that goes with it. I just want to play the game. We've come a long way in the national rankings, and we get better every year.

Back home, in Zabella, a realm accessible through a rift gate near Romania, I'm still the commander of the werewolf king's army, with Benny as my second, but I left my lead lieutenant in charge of keeping them in line and training any new recruits in my absence. I've given over five hundred years, and so much more, to our military and our people. I need this. The distance. The release. The escape. The nightmares came with me, of course, but I'd probably be lost without them too.

The team finished drills hours ago, but I still had restlessly angry energy that I needed to keep working off. So, it's just me and the ice. I pump my legs as hard as they'll go, leaning my body through the turns in the rink. *It's too bad hockey rinks aren't the size of football fields.* I bet I could have one built somewhere. The guys would love that. The pack probably would too. If I had it built on the pack lands, everyone would have somewhere quiet to skate where they could work their frustrations out as well. Not even just frustrations, but any restlessness, especially the energetic pups.

I can't believe I've already been the Alpha of the Great Lakes Pack for nearly fifty years. Leading a growing pack is so much different than commanding an army, but there are also similarities. The army is all strict order and physical exertion. The pack is so much more. It's family. Real family.

My father hated pack life and was too busy kissing royal asses to ever even entertain being a more active part of our world. The life a werewolf lives in Zabella is different than in this realm. While there are a few packs, since everyone is werewolf, it's much like the older human civilizations. Living in village communities across the land, governed by different Alphas that all answer to the king.

Growing up with just my father after my mother died was a cold and lonely existence. My mother was my light. She was my warmth. Everyone she encountered seemed to have no choice but to love her. Her energy was infectious, but she was too light for this world. My father's world. He is darkness. I wouldn't be surprised if his father was the devil himself. He is cold and detached, and he cares for no one but himself. His name and reputation are all that ever have or ever will matter. It's what led to my sweet mother's death.

She would have loved the pack that my men and I built. My closest men came to this realm with me. Once the decision was made, we packed our belongings, crossed the rift gate, came to the states, and landed in the Great Lakes area. We settled in the Shawnee State Forest, and the pack just kind of happened. Other wolves slowly made their way to us, some coming from Zabella to live among humans and others that were already here. They came seeking shelter, protection, and a pack. As long as they were hardworking and honest, they were allowed to stay.

I'm shaken from my thoughts, still barreling around the rink, as my men burst through the doors separating the rink from the rest of the arena, squabbling about something I don't care enough to listen in on. Benny flags me down, and I make my way over. While Benny is my second in command of the army, it extends to all things. He's also been my best friend my entire life; he's my pack Beta, and he's my left wing on the ice. I wouldn't be the man I am without him. He grounds me. When my darkness takes over and it feels like all light has left the world, he can always find me and bring me back. He's also an idiot and doesn't know when to just shut the fuck up, most of the time.

"Do you realize you've had your walls up forever? No one really needs anything, but I'm bored, and the twins are driving Slate crazy," Benny hollers as I near the edge of the ice.

"If you weren't so loud and ever stopped talking, I wouldn't have to block you," I snap back as I drop onto the bench to remove my skates.

He's having a tantrum because he never grew out of the stage that pups go through where nothing in this world can shut them up, which means I get tired of listening. So, I erect mental walls to block out communication.

As a pack, anyone can communicate with each other telepathically within the same realm. Because our communication is telepathic, distance doesn't matter as long as you're within the same plane of existence. While it's an amazing gift, sometimes it just gets too loud in my head, and I need some time with only my thoughts. I can't imagine having to have those stupid phones stuck to my ear all the time just to communicate like humans do. They don't even work half the time, especially in the state parks and forests where most werewolf packs reside.

He wasn't exaggerating, though. I don't know what Eris and Dolos are on about, but Slate really does look ready to murder them, while Andrei looks bored with the whole mess. Shaking my head, I shout at my Omegas, "What is it now? What is so important that you're tempting your fate?"

The cheshire grins on their faces never mean good things. Raising one eyebrow, I look to Andrei for any sign of what's going on, but his passive expression clearly shows how little he cares. By the time I reach the twins, they're nearly bouncing on their toes as they reply, "We might have accidentally stolen Slate's girl."

Scrubbing my hand down my face, I mumble, "Do I even want to know? Slate, is this really about some chick again?"

Turning to face him, he shakes his head and says, "Nah, Boss. I was mad for all of a second, but they can have her. She's not my mate, so she doesn't mean anything to me. They just won't shut the fuck up." He stands now, still spewing his frustrations, "They're the ones that wanted to share her, and I don't know how many times I've told them, I don't want in on their nasty shit."

I chuckle at first, but he wasn't joking; the twins won't shut up about it. "Look, we really don't want to hear about your nasty sexcapades and whatever you weirdos do when you share a woman," I say with my back to my men, replacing my skates with shoes. They don't seem to have even heard me, as they're steadily arguing louder and louder.

ENOUGH!

All four men immediately lower their heads, Eris releasing a small whimper. I don't have to use my Alpha energy on my men often, but the twins are professionals when it comes to bringing it out of me. "You are all full-grown men, and I will not referee your bullshit. Eris and Dolos, keep your weird shit to yourselves. Unless you want to be knocked on your ass, you'll figure it out. You're acting like teenage, human females." Grabbing my skates, I turn towards the locker room without another word.

I've been in the shower all of five minutes when Benny swings around the corner with that stupid smile on his face. "You seem especially irritable today. What's up?" he asks.

I just shake my head, turning up the heat of the water, hoping it can drown out the anger. The pain. The past. "Nothing's up," I reply when I realize he won't leave until I say something.

I've barely made it through the door of our home before I immediately want to leave. I hear India raging at someone over the phone about scuffing her shoes at a photo shoot. I can't imagine screaming at someone over a scuffed-fucking-shoe and I just can't deal with her today.

I stop just inside the door, not wanting to go further. The guys file in moments after. Walking past me, the twins throw me a look that says they're off to see if they can enrage her enough to make her leave, and in this moment, I'm thankful for these two royal pains in my ass.

India is the daughter of the king's advisor, and we're arranged to be married at some time in the, hopefully distant, future. Sometimes, very rarely, she really isn't that bad, but most of the time she's a raging bitch. I hold on to the hope that she finds her mate, and I don't have to go through with this. She's attractive by human standards, but it's as fake as she is. I don't understand how she can be so full of herself and yet hate herself so much that she has to constantly get work done on her face. She only buys or wears the most expensive, name-brand items. The human men stop and literally drool over her.

She knows her marriage to me will be nothing romantic, but that doesn't stop her from occasionally trying to move our relationship to depths we agreed it wouldn't go. When we were first informed of our betrothal, I did not have any say in the decision.

India and I have not spoken much regarding our impending arrangement. I made it clear early on that I did not have feelings for her in that way. Our relationship would only be a partnership. She's continued to push those boundaries for years, and to this day, I still do not have romantic feelings for her like she does for me.

I'm also not happy with the fact that she will be the Luna of my pack with the marriage. I've only taken her to my pack once because of how she acted while we were there. She wouldn't stop complaining that her pointy-ass shoes were sinking into the ground. She was not warm or kind to any women or pups. She started commenting on all the improvements she would need if she were forced to stay there. A Luna is supposed to be a proud leader of her people. A Luna should be someone they can look up to and count on.

Our fathers arranged the marriage because of my position in Zabella. The advisor's daughter and the commander of the army. It looks good on paper, but it's not what I want. India is happy with it because being my wife would raise her status even further.

We are able to satisfy each other physically on occasion,

but what we do couldn't be further from making love. Our sex is hard and angry. Just me releasing the frustration of my past and future, and she meets me blow for blow. I didn't want to take our relationship to that level and give her a false sense of what I could bring to our future marriage, but she made it clear that she understood that this is just all I'm capable of. This is all I have left.

Stepping into my office, I kick the door shut behind me and sink into my large leather chair. *Brutus, pack status update.* We're three to four hours away from the pack here in Mogadore. Close enough that we can get there quickly when needed, but far enough that the pack has the peace they need from the media surrounding the hockey team, and such.

Nothing urgent to report, Alpha. We welcomed a new pack member today. Mum and pup are healthy and resting. The hunters brought back enough meat to last us another couple of weeks.

I'm thankful we built the pack with a solid foundation that allows us to be away for hockey and not have to worry about how the pack is doing.

Thank you, Brutus. Make sure Mackenzie and her new pup have everything they need from us; it's her firstborn, and I know Rodger is worried about her. See if one of the den mothers wouldn't mind spending some time with them. Let me know if anything comes up.

Stretching as I stand, I head over to my small bar in the corner and pour half a glass of my favorite whiskey. It's the best human-whiskey I've found. It's not worth the hassle to bring ours in from home.

Just as my thighs hit the chair again, the door slowly swings open to reveal India. Her white-blonde-dyed hair is pulled into a long, sleek ponytail so tight that I don't know how she can move her face. She looks at me with a strained smile and saunters toward me in a way that says she's hoping I need to let off some steam this evening. With how shitty I feel, I would normally send her away, but maybe it would make me feel better, or at least take the edge off.

She perches herself on my right thigh, looking down at me with big, green eyes that get her pretty much anything from everyone else she crosses paths with. Even I would find her green eyes gorgeous, but there is something that lies beneath them that I just can't put my finger on. It's unsettling.

I don't react or speak, just a simple curt nod. She visibly melts, thinking she's gotten her way this time, so I'll let her have her moment. She shuffles out of the room, and I can hear her nearly sprinting to my room at the end of the hall.

I allow myself another few moments of peace to finish my whiskey before following after her. Almost to my bedroom, I hear Benny. *I recommend everyone clear out. Alpha's headed to take some steam out on India again. Alpha, please remember to block this time; nobody wants in on that. Well, the twins might never . . .* I throw my walls up before he can finish his thought. They know how our arrangement works. They also know that I hope I never actually have to marry her. I've been trying to find a way out of it for years.

India has spent her life living as an American socialite for so long that I think she forgets she's a werewolf. She does the social media thing on her phone, obsessed with every click, like, and follow. I think she calls herself an influencer or something. The thought of her influencing anyone, about anything, is unfathomable. Part of our arrangement is that our impending betrothal does not carry into our public lives. To the world, we're both single. In private, and in Zabella, we'll be married someday.

She's already naked on my bed with my blankets wrapped around her when I enter the room.

"Turn around, hands and knees on the bed," I order as I begin removing my clothing. She knows better than to argue with me when I'm like this. She tried once, resulting in my clothes being returned to my body and her leaving town for a couple weeks. I need the control, and I need the release.

I take my time, making her wait, knowing how much she hates the quiet anticipation, but also knowing it makes her even wetter. Without ceremony, I climb onto the bed behind her, my wolf growling under my skin—he hates her with a strength I don't understand. In a swift single motion, I grip her hips and fully seat myself inside her. She cries out from the intrusion, and my wolf's low growl becomes a snarl.

Her moaning whimpers only fuel me more as I pound into her without restraint, urging me to take her harder. My release finds me quickly, but I don't let it enter her body. Instead, I unload it all in her hair, knowing how much she hates it. She complains about how hard it is to wash out. I smirk at myself for the first time today. I'm not a total fucking monster, though. Reaching both arms around her lean frame, my left hand pinches her nipple, while my right hand travels lower. Once I've reached her mound, I begin to pump two fingers into her while my palm rubs her bundle of nerves until she swiftly finds her release as well.

I roll around her to drop onto my pillow, lost in thought. I hate to admit that I do feel a little better after hashing it out with India. I guess if I'm forced to marry someone, it helps when that someone can handle me and the demons from my past. I feel myself drifting off to sleep as she crawls out of bed, heading for the bathroom to shower and wash me out of her hair.

I know I'm dreaming as soon as it begins.

It's the same every time.

I'm almost home when I hear her screaming.

I immediately shift into my wolf and bolt for our small home on the furthest edge of the castle grounds. Even on four legs, it feels as though an eternity passes before I make it to our cottage.

Shifting back into my human body and throwing the door off the hinges as I burst through, I'm met with silence, which is far more terrifying. At least when she was screaming, I knew she was alive. She's been having that itchy feeling lately, like someone's watching her. I know it doesn't make sense, but I learned a long time ago to trust her judgment; I couldn't find any trace of anyone. No scents. No tracks. Nothing.

I finally find her just outside the back door after frantically searching every room. She's lying face down in her new clusters of azaleas. She planted them when she realized she was pregnant with our pup. I slowly kneel to turn her over, but I already know.

I can't feel her wolf, and mine is already howling. Her heartbeat is so light and slow that I know she only has a moment left, so I do the only thing I can. I hold her as close to me as physically possible and whisper all the words I hope she can hear in her final moments in her body.

As our mate bond is snapped, the scream that rips from my lungs is unnatural. It's what I imagine a dragon would sound like if they still walked the earth. I know that there's little chance the baby survived, as it wasn't due for another month. Holding my breath, I lay my head on the tight swell of her belly and listen and pray to the Moon Goddess that at least one can be saved. Silence. I've never understood when someone said they found silence to be loud. I know now, and I wish I could take away this knowledge.

BENNY! I know he and my other men would have heard me scream, but I need to make sure. I may be the stronger of the two of us, but he's the tracker. I need him.

BENNNYYY! I scream once more as his cinnamon-colored wolf hurtles into view, howling and crying immediately as he takes in the scene. He's off and running before I even have to ask; he knows what I need. So I just hold them. My Imogen. My mate. My reason for living and breathing. My world. And my child.

I don't know how long I sit in the same spot, just holding them as tightly to my body as they can go. Benny returns, slowly approaching us. He loved her as much as I did. He shifts, drops to his haunches, and wraps his arms around us. We sit there like that for only another moment. Benny sits up, looks at me, and says, "The guys are on the way. I'm so sorry, Roman. I couldn't find anything; not a single trace of anyone being here at all." I think I can stand and step away from her as my father comes into sight just before the rest of my men.

"ARE YOU HAPPY NOW?" I roar. My whole body is trembling with rage and the effects of losing my mate. The one soul in the universe made just for me. My other half.

My father always hated her and felt she was beneath me. How can anything so perfect be measured by levels of status?

Who the fuck cares that she grew up in the village like a normal werewolf and not some royal pompous ass?!

He holds his hands out in front of him as if to surrender. "I mean no harm. I heard and came to check on you. Oh, son, I'm so sorry."

I can't hear him over the roaring of my blood and the howling of my wolf as I crumble back down to the ground. *I can't do this.* Another guttural cry leaves my human body.

I can't do this. I release control to my wolf, who is still howling. The howls morph into snarling at my father as he backs away and finally leaves my sight. As my men approach, I wrap my wolf's body around her. Blood coating my thick, cream-colored fur. Her blood.

I hadn't even noticed the blood before.

My wolf can't handle it either, and I'm thrown back into my human form, screaming and praying that this is also my end and I can be with them on the other side.

I'm still screaming as I jolt awake in the dark. My entire body is covered in a sheen of cold sweat. India lets out a small screech as she holds onto me in the night. "Oh, Roman baby, are you ok? You're shaking."

"Don't touch me!" I shout as I throw her arm away from my body and launch myself out of the bed. "You know not to touch me when it comes to her."

She bows her head, dresses quickly, and leaves.

You okay, Boss? Benny asks in my mind. My wolf is still howling, so I let him know I'm going to go let him run it off.

As the sun rises, I'm still running.

I'm still running because I can still feel her in my arms, almost five hundred years later. I can still hear the roaring silence of the moment her heart stopped beating. I can still feel the moment the bond snapped. I can still feel the moment my world stopped spinning and they were gone.

3
Leera

Waking up the next day in a new place should be weird, but since I've been doing it my whole life, the only weird part is that my parents aren't here. I know they're with me in spirit and all that, but not having them physically here is still so strange. I no longer wake up to the smell of Mom's coffee in the air, while Dad complains about her stinking the whole house up. It's the little things I miss the most.

I reach over and grab my phone off my bedside table. I have a text from my new roommate.

When we were assigned to our dorms, we were given our roommates contact information with the option to communicate. I chose to tentatively reach out and test the water. After all, I would be living with this person after only ever living with my parents. Not to mention I've never really had a chance to make friends, so I'm hopeful Zoey and I can continue to build a relationship. If not friends, at least amicable acquaintances, but hopefully friends. So far, we've hit it off pretty well. We like a lot of the same things, and we've been in constant communication since I texted her that first day.

Zozo

Hey Leera – I don't think I'm gonna make it today!

Since my parents planned this whole surprise road trip shebang it's taking longer to make the drive to campus.

Hey Zoey – no rush! Have fun!

What I wouldn't give to be on a last-hoorah-before-college road trip with my parents.

Well, now that she won't be here today, I have some time to explore. I hop out of bed and pick out some cute but comfy clothes. Pink is my go-to just because it's my favorite color and it makes me happy. It also looks so good with my silver hair. I tie it all up in an obnoxious, messy bun on top of my head, pulling bitty strands out by my ears on a reflex. We never found out why my hair was so prematurely silver, but I've chosen to embrace it. Plus, it looks killer with my ice-blue eyes, and who am I to argue with nature?

I'm kind of glad I have this day to myself. The campus is even nicer than I expected. When I looked up the college and the surrounding area, it seemed kind of old and run-down. Although, in person, it's really not that bad. Sure, it's a little old; a lot of colleges and universities are, but they keep it clean, and the landscapers take their job very seriously. I haven't seen a flower or blade of grass out of place.

The school colors are red, white, and gold, and I love that they've incorporated school-colored flowers everywhere. Something so simple brings out just a little extra sunshine and happiness. I love flowers. Flowers of all kinds. They're all so beautiful, colorful, and unique. While Mom and Dad were always photographing mostly animals, I would gravitate towards the flora and fauna native to the given area.

The natural beauty of things has always just amazed me. It's always blown my mind how the most strange and beautiful things simply exist with no one regularly caring for them. From cacti to flowers and trees, it all just speaks to me, and I can't get enough.

After I finished ogling all the floral arrangements, I found a cute little coffee shop on the corner of campus that makes the yummiest iced coffee I think I've ever had. You would miss it if you weren't paying close attention.

There's a little strip of shops, and it's almost hidden between the collegiate gear shop called Swag and a textbook shop with a giant sign that just says BOOKS. Each of those storefronts is so full of sale racks and signs that you could easily miss the entrance tucked into the alcove.

The door is all glass and covered in window chalk. There are smiley faces, flowers, hearts, and coffee cups painted all over the door. Right in the middle, in funky lettering, it says Cool Beans. I didn't know which flavor to try, so I got one called Wheece's. It was a white chocolate peanut butter combination that tasted like heaven. I knew I'd have to come back and try all the flavors! The barista was a nice girl who looked to be around my age. *Does she go to school here too? Maybe we could be friends? Oh! Maybe if I have the time and energy, once I get settled, maybe I could work here too!*

I spend the rest of the day wandering around, familiarizing myself with the buildings, places to eat, and potential study spots.

I chose photojournalism as my major. I loved the life I lived with my parents, so why not keep living that life as an adult? My hope is that one day I can be even a fraction of the photojournalists my parents were. Maybe travel the world and see even more of nature's beauty.

Zoey is majoring in photography, so we should have some classes together. She's also here on a full-ride scholarship, like me. I know it shouldn't matter, but it makes me feel better that my roommate isn't some excessively wealthy social elitist. I'm not broke or anything, by any means. Mom and Dad both . . . they . . . they both had—*deep breath in, hold it, release*—they both had life insurance to make sure I was taken care of. I'd give the money back to have them back any day. I don't WANT this money. I never even knew they were covered for stuff like that. I'm sure it was all Dad's doing.

It's finally getting easier and easier to think about them, but every now and then, the grief and anxiety hit me like a tidal wave. I'm forever grateful my therapist gave me the tools I needed to understand how to survive those waves of emotion and come out on the other side.

The next morning, I'm woken by the door to my dorm being opened and whispering voices filling the space. Peeking over my shoulder, I find Zoey and her parents trying to move things quietly into the small dorm room.

"It's okay, I was starting to wake up," I try to say without my voice sounding like gravel from sleep. Zoey lets out a small squeal, bounds straight to my bed, and wraps her arms around me like we'd done it a hundred times. "I'm so sorry we woke you, but I'm so excited to see you! Wow, your hair really is silver. How much upkeep does that take?" she said with a contagious smile on her face. I loved that she rambled a little, since I had a tendency to ramble a lot. I feel like every little thing we have in common can help a new friendship take off on the right foot.

I rub my eyes as I sit up, followed by stretching my arms above my head. "Good morning, Zoey and Zoey's parents," I half yawn.

"Good morning!" they all reply cheerily at the same time.

"I'll just get dressed, and maybe we could grab some coffee before getting Zoey all moved in?" I asked as I rummaged through my drawers for what I'd wear today.

Zoey spoke for everyone, bouncing on her toes. "That sounds perfect!"

You could tell Zoey's parents weren't really ready to leave her when the time came. They'd stalled at every opportunity today, and now that it was getting dark out, they were really leaving, and they were struggling.

How would my parents have handled a day like this? Moving me in? Leaving me without them for the first time in my life? Shaking the somber thoughts from my head, I let them have their moment. I head over to the small cabinet over my desk and take my vitamins, making a mental note that I've got two months left, so I'll need to figure out where to get them myself afterwards.

Out of the corner of my vision, Zoey finally closes the door and wipes at her teary eyes for a minute before slapping her smile on her face and making her way towards me. I wonder if that's a new-person smile to make friends or if she really smiles like that all the time. I hope it's all the time because it makes me want to smile too.

Zoey is radiant. Not just visually, but her energy too. Being around her just makes you want to be happy. She's quite a bit taller than me, probably five foot five, give or take. She has long, straight black hair, nearly reaching her waist, and gray eyes that give away her every thought. She also has the cutest little heart-shaped birthmark on her jawline.

"So, what should we do with our first official evening as best friends?" she asks as she plops down on the edge of my bed. The shock only lasts a second before I regain use of my brain.

"B-best friends?" I ask with watery eyes.

"Well duh! I mean, we've been talking all summer, we have loads in common, we had a great day together, and we live together for the foreseeable future. I don't have any friends here either, so unless you're secretly like a serial killer or something, then yes, we'll be best friends, so why not label this thing now?"

This time I initiate the hug and nod into her shoulder, "I'd like that very much."

We said we were going to watch Twilight and snack, but we've talked through the whole thing, and now the credits are rolling. What an amazing night, though. I knew everything would be okay, but this is better than okay. It's great. It's more than I ever expected.

4
ROMAN

We've only got a couple of months before the season starts back up and I'm on edge. Practicing hockey isn't the same as playing hockey, even scrimmaging with the team can't take the edge off. I need the roar of the crowd, slamming men I don't care about into the walls, and winning. It's the only thing that can quiet my mind and the demons who take residence in my thoughts.

On the plus side, the team has come a long way and we're looking really good this year. I don't know if we'll take the Stanley Cup, but we should definitely make it to the playoffs. We've been especially hard on Slate. He's the goalie and he really is the best for the job, but he has a couple weaknesses that the other teams had started to notice and exploit. So, we spent a lot of the off season watching his bottom right corner and pissing him off. He plays worse when he's in a bad mood. If the other team gets him worked up enough, all he can focus on is how he would murder them if given the chance, and he forgets all about the game. Luckily, while the twins are my Omegas and can bring lightness to heavy situations, they can also be the most infuriating jackasses I've ever encountered. So naturally, they've taken their job of pissing off Slate very seriously.

Benny has been spending his time bouncing back and forth between trying to keep me levelheaded and building bridges with Andrei. Andrei is the newest member of my trusted men, both in hockey and with the pack. He came to us angry and broken, and that's something I understand, and we bonded through it. It is strange having someone so young around all the time. Andrei is only eighteen years old, but since werewolves grow so much faster and larger than humans, you can't tell he's not a twenty-something-year-old man.

Pain will do that to anyone, though, and you can tell he carries a desire for vengeance. Benny wants him to be more, though. He wants to push him out of the lone wolf vibes he still exudes at times. If anyone can get him through it, it's Benny.

I finish lacing up my skates and make my way to the ice. Coach and the team are waiting for me and a couple other stragglers. Coach is a big old werewolf who was the best of his time on the ice. He's an even bigger ass than me, but with a heart of gold. He acts like the Alpha of the men and families of the team, taking care of us all. I had forgotten what it felt like to be taken care of, and it's nice. I would never tell him or any other soul, but he's been more of a father to me than my own ever was.

"Alright boys, we've still got work to do if you're done being a bunch of pussies!" Coach thunders at everyone, which means it's time to start drills.

After an hour of drills we'll start running the plays, followed by scrimmaging, ending with more cool down drills. He runs us hard, but he knows what we need—me especially. I'm pretty sure he's researched how to torture men with hockey drills. Then I swear he takes his research, tries it out on us, then amps it up to make sure we wish we were dead. Even if sometimes I still need to skate it off after practice, most of the team nearly crawls off the ice. The newbies are always begging for death at the end of their first week.

As practice ends today, I don't feel the need to keep going so I hit the showers with the rest of the team. Everyone else is amped up for our opening game and there is an infectious thrill coursing through the air. The first game is against my biggest rival, on and off the ice—the Augusta Vultures.

Their Team Captain is Khaos Mokotoff, Alpha of the New England Pack, and my lifelong rival. He was born a year after I was, and our fathers constantly pinned us against each other. Inciting challenges and forcing us to compete with each other over every little thing, causing the rift to begin young.

Being a year older, I was always a step ahead and a little bit stronger. The one time I ever lost to him, my father beat me so badly he had to call a healer. I never lost again.

He was also Imogen's brother. While he and his father were considered upper class, Imogen was not. Khaos' father was a shit mate and prowled around searching the villages for women in heat, and thus, Imogen was born. The scandal was mostly kept under wraps until Khaos ran into her. He felt the family bond with her and approached her. I had never really seen him happy until he found her. He spent all his extra time with her. He'd sneak her and her mother food, clothing and money every chance he had.

Khaos and my father were furious that we were mates. Khaos didn't want her to be subjected to any of the bullshit that came along with being a part of the royal world. My father demanded I reject her as my mate, just because she lived in the village instead of being part of the noble circles.

Khaos still blames me for her death. That's about all we can agree on. So, we take it out on the ice. The league doesn't know the specifics, but they know when they put us together there are always fireworks, and the crowd just eats it up.

Back home that evening, everything is uncomfortably quiet. The guys all went out to get rip-roaring drunk and I'm just not in the mood. I can't pinpoint what's going on with me, but something feels off. It has for about a couple weeks now. Like something is coming, something big, but I can't tell if it's good or bad. India hasn't been around lately, so at least I have that to be thankful for.

Since we've got the weekend off, I let the guys know I'm going to head to the pack and check on everyone. A nice long run there, being able to feel needed for a day, and a long run back, will do me good. I take my clothes off and drop them in the laundry room for Matilda, our housekeeper. If I destroy any more clothes right now, she's going to pummel me. She may be smaller and older but don't let that sweet little old lady act fool you, she can hold her own.

My wolf surges forward without a second thought. Wild cream-colored fur sprouts all over my body as my bones crunch and realign accordingly. Even after so many centuries, the whole process still amazes me.

When I do visit, I like to arrive at the pack unannounced and at odd and different times. I want to ensure security is doing their job and keeping everyone safe. I approach with my thoughts blocked so they don't hear me, but I immediately feel the presence of someone. Just as Brutus calls out, "I can smell you Alpha but nice try!"

Shifting back, I accept the cloak in his outstretched hand. "Brutus what are you doing on duty tonight?" I ask, curious as to why my fill-in leader of the pack has resorted to working a security shift.

"Ah just covering for Rodger. You remember they had their pup and he's taken a more active parenting role than most. We wanted to embrace it and let him enjoy these moments."

Nodding I clasp him on the shoulder in greeting. "I agree with your decision. I don't want our pack to uphold prehistoric notions and cease to grow and evolve. Make sure they have everything they need. Anything else to report?"

He shakes his head and tells me of all the day to day normalcy that's taken place in my absence. If they don't have anything for me to do, I'll have to come up with something. We may even research that giant ice rink I was thinking about. Either way I'm going to enjoy this day with my pack before I head back for the city tomorrow.

As we make our way into the common area of the pack homes, people of all ages come out to say hello. It's still strange to be in charge of people in this way. For so long, leading the army, it was all brute strength and order. It wasn't a family.

Our pack has grown so much that we've almost reached a point that we're going need to build more pack houses. They're nothing fancy by any means, but each family has their own cottage style home with all the necessary amenities. I splurged a little bit, a couple years ago, and built a clubhouse for the pack. It's got a gym, a movie theater, a sauna, a pool for the summer months, and a playground for the pups.

Just as the thought crosses my mind, my ears are assaulted by about a dozen little voices coming my way. One of my favorite things about our pack is all the pups. They come running at me in both forms. Some in their human form and others in their wolf form. Seeing how happy and well taken care of they are brings me the greatest sense of pride.

I couldn't keep our pup safe; I will make sure these children never know of those struggles.

As they reach me, I'm tackled to the ground. Hands and feet and paws are everywhere. Laughing while they giggle and attack me. I roll over, lift myself to my knees and toss Brutus my cloak.

In an instant I release my wolf. I'm hopping around and nuzzling them. Hopping turns into wrestling for nearly an hour. The parents begin to gather their young ones when there's only one little girl left. She's so small, she's probably only three or four years old. She reaches her little body onto her tip toes, takes my snout in both of her tiny little hands, and pulls me into a hug that I didn't know I needed. "Good boy," is all she says, and then she's skipping away to her parents.

Shifting back, and pulling the cloak back on, I'm feeling lighter than I have in ages.

The rest of the day passes mostly uneventfully. I talk with Brutus about all the new developments within the pack, which isn't much. We go over some requests that the pack had and make plans to bring them to life.

Some of the older boys, and probably the men, requested a basketball court. The woman requested a paved track around the property for them to walk the little ones in strollers, skate, and ride bikes.

Just because we're werewolves it doesn't mean we want to live like animals all the time. Well, a few people do sometimes, but to each their own.

The day goes by so quickly that it feels like I've barely arrived when I notice the sun beginning its descent. Walking back to the edge of our lands, I hand Brutus my cloak, and take back off towards home, still thinking about that sweet little girl and all the pups. They make all of it worthwhile.

5
Leera

College is a whole new world. I spent the weeks before class started just getting a feel of the area and getting used to being around so many people all the time.

While I was able to do a lot of exploring of the grounds, the real wonder set in when classes finally began and I got to look around inside more of the buildings. Like the outsides, they kept the old, historic look going but obviously kept up well with the maintenance and paint to keep it looking sparkly clean. You can see the inspiration for some of the older European structures in their designs. While my parents' work was focused around nature and wildlife, we made time to see the sights in the areas we traveled too.

Though most of the buildings had lots of historic features from the time they were built, they kept up with modern needs as well. There were LED screens scattered through the halls, advertising different teams and clubs. The old concrete floors had a fresh, waxy shine to them. There were even electronic charging stations with the cords already available for anyone who needed a quick charge; they kind of looked like the little stands you see in airports.

The buzz of the narrow hallways full of people was also a completely new experience for me, as I had never been to school. The first couple of days were really overwhelming, and I had to work myself out of a panic attack.

Once I got a little more used to it, my body relaxed into the routine. I had to convince myself that I wasn't being ambushed for no reason; this was just how it was between classes when everyone was just working on getting from one place to another. It wasn't like this before classes began because everyone was just kind of meandering around like I was. Now everyone is always in a rush, and it's just so loud.

Zoey's and my immediate connection hasn't faded, and I will forever be grateful to the universe for giving her to me after feeling so alone. We spend all of our extra time together studying, trying food from all the different restaurants on campus, drinking coffee, and watching our favorite comfort movies.

When classes started, I was super stressed out about how to go about all of this. I know college is new for everyone, but almost everyone else went to school while I was traveling the world with my parents. I still don't regret growing up that way, but the acclimation process was heavier than I anticipated. I never thought I was missing out on anything, but looking back now, maybe I was, and I never really acknowledged it.

We're a couple weeks into school now, and I think I've gathered a decent grasp on things. My favorite class is my Intro to Photography class that I have with Zoey. The professor is kind and animated, and he makes us laugh. We're still in the throes of all the boring parts of class, but I can't wait to really hit the ground running.

I'm thankful for Zoey for more than just our friendship. She is such a social butterfly and doesn't seem to know much about stranger danger. She can carry on a conversation with anyone about anything. Mostly, I just observe from the background, but she has managed to pull me into a few colorful conversations. She's made it her personal mission to help me become better at socializing. It looks so easy when she does it, but my words get caught in my throat, and I curl in on myself. Mom and Dad always made it look easy, too. We didn't engage with a lot of people, but they handled it a lot like Zoey does. The way she easily volleys the conversation back and forth, smoothly transitioning between topics of conversation, is its own form of art that I'd like to learn.

My photojournalism class is more my speed. It's calmer and quieter, and Professor Sinclair is a small woman with warm ebony skin, kind eyes, and wildly fun natural hair. Her approach to teaching is also more in line with the way I work. She doesn't drill us quite so hard with the technical side of things that we can read about in our textbooks. She believes that to truly learn and grow in your skills, you have to do the work.

To reinforce her feelings on this, she's throwing us to the wolves right out of the gate. There are a ton of sports teams in the area. Between the professional teams, the college teams, and multiple sports seasons overlapping, there is apparently a lot going on. My parents and I were never sporty people in the way that some people have favorite teams or know all the rules. I'm going to have to do a lot of my own research on this assignment as well. I guess with all the different sports going on, some teams are finishing their season already, some are in the off-season, and others are getting ready to kick off a new season.

Professor Sinclair was able to secure enough press badges and appointments for each of us to interview and photograph a team for our first big assignment. A lot of the guys and locals in class know exactly who they want to interview, but it was harder for me. My dad watched the big sports finales, like the Superbowl and the World Cup, I think it's called, but we were animal and nature people, so I never got into the whole organized sports hype.

After my research, I decided I wanted a sport that was about to start. I felt like the interview would be calmer in preparation for a season to begin than it would be at the end of one, or if I tried to jump into something mid-season. That way, I could maybe also follow the team, learn the game, and continue to use the same team for future assignments. I know I'm getting a little ahead of myself, but that's my dad's planning side shining through. This led me to choose hockey. Apparently, this local professional team was a pretty big deal; I signed up for that one along with most of the class.

Today was the day Professor Sinclair was handing out our chosen assignments. We had to write a paper explaining why we should get the team we wanted, our planned interviews, and our intentions. We were also asked to write about ourselves. Who we were before college and what we hoped to gain from our education. I felt like my paper was more about my parents than me, but it also portrayed all the things I needed people to understand about me.

As class ended, we were all still anxiously awaiting our assignments. It looked like everyone else, like me, expected to be told at the beginning of the class so we could start planning, but she had other ideas. Nearing the end of class, Professor Sinclair finally gathered our attention. "As I call your name, you will come to the front, accept your assignments, and you are then dismissed for the day. I know we had a lot of people sign up for the same teams. I want no trading, bickering, or foul attitudes. You will not always get the assignments you want in your career, and those should be handled with the same diligence and respect as your first choice."

Everyone just nodded.

She began calling names. Some people were pleased with themselves, while others were clearly trying to mask their disappointment. She wasn't calling us in any particular order. I didn't know when it would be my turn, but I would apparently be all the way down the line. I wasn't used to that either. With the last name Adams, I was used to being called first or close to it.

I was the last one left in the room when Professor Sinclair called me to the front with tears in her eyes. *Oh no, please, no more pity.*

"Leera, when I saw your name on my roster, I wouldn't allow myself to believe it was you," she said, looking at my assignment in her hands.

"I'm sorry, ma'am. I don't understand," I said low and uncomfortably.

She shook her head as if trying to fling away forgotten memories. "I went to university with your parents. They were my best friends. After they had you, they became quite reclusive, and I didn't hear or see from them as much, but I always followed their career."

Whatever I had thought she would say could never amount to the words she left hanging in the air. I found myself again unable to form a response. A large knot of emotion lodged itself in my throat and I begged myself not to get upset. She seemed to notice my discomfort, shook off her own emotion, and returned to her quiet bubbly self.

"I'm sorry, Leera. I was so upset when I heard about their deaths, but I want you to know I'm here if you need anything. I gave you the assignment you asked for, but I made you last on my list so we could talk about it and no one would get worked up over it. I didn't give you the assignment you requested because of your parents, though. I gave it to you based on the assignment. The written explanations I requested from you all were kind of like job applications. Your application was the best for the job. You'll be covering Mogadore's hockey team. Your interview is scheduled for next week. The coach and the starting six players have agreed to meet with you."

I so badly wanted to say thank you, but my body wouldn't allow it. I nodded and made eye contact, hoping my eyes said *thank you* for me, and walked out the door. I kept walking until I found my favorite study spot under the weeping willow tree. I slowly sank to the ground and focused on trying to calm my aching heart.

I don't know how much time had passed, but I was feeling more myself and had processed all the information to the best of my ability. I didn't want to act differently with Professor Sinclair because I didn't want anyone to think she was playing favorites with me. I also didn't know her. But I could get to know her and have another person in my corner. Right now, I need to focus on my assignment. A lot of people will be upset that I am assigned to work with the Predators, which is why I am going to have to prove myself.

I pull myself to my feet, grab all my stuff off the ground, walk over to Cool Beans to grab an afternoon pick-me-up, and head back to our room. I have an interview to plan. This interview, if I handle it right, could set me up on my projects for this class, and possibly my photography class, for quite a bit of the year, maybe even longer. Hell, I might even find a love for hockey.

6
ROMAN

If she doesn't leave soon, I'm going to be an ass and throw her out. I'm trying really hard not to be a dick, but I've lost all my patience.

India has been here for two days. She's kissing everyone's asses and playing nice, and it's weirding the guys out, especially the twins. It's weirding me the fuck out too, if I'm being honest. I know it's just an act after our last interaction, and she's just trying to get my good graces, but it's not that simple.

I don't hate her. I hate that I'm being forced to marry someone I don't enjoy spending time with. Someone I can't see taking care of our people. It's really just annoying me more than anything. She's been prancing around the townhouse all day, pretending to be some kind of housewife, if I had to guess. Now she's been in the kitchen for hours and had better not be upsetting Matilda. Those two have had quite a few spats in the last few years.

She's so dead set on being accepted; she let everyone know she was going to make us a big family meal to have tonight. Multiple courses, a coordinated wine menu, a set time—the works. I don't know what she's up to, but it can't be good. Just as I'm getting up to head to the table, I hear the doorbell. Not expecting anyone to be here for me, I stay my course for the large dining room. If I were a better man, I'd go to the kitchen to see if India needed or wanted my help with anything. But I'm not. All that was good in me died with Imogen and our child. I take my seat at the head of the table and pour myself a glass of the red wine that is set on the bar that runs along the wall beside the table.

Just as the glass grazes my lips, Matilda comes around the corner, looking sheepish and upset. I'm on my feet in a moment. "Matilda, what's wrong?"

She raises her hands slightly with a small shake of her head. "Master Razboinic, you have a guest," she says as strongly as she can muster. I want to question her more; she never addresses me as master, just as his scent hits me. *It all makes sense.*

Benny, grab the guys and get your asses to the dining room now. I'm able to finish my thought to Benny just as my father strolls into the room like he owns the place. I should have known. Now the question is, did India invite him or did he arrange the whole thing and demand she orchestrate it on his behalf?

"Father," I grunt, trying to seem unphased by his presence. Just looking at him sets my blood to boil. He's probably an inch shorter than my six-foot-six frame, but he still manages to look down his nose at me. We have the same square jaw, but that's where our similarities end. His dark hair is slicked back and plastered to his head with what has to be an entire bottle of some kind of hair product, where my sandy hair is just long enough to either look like a mess or be styled just right. He's broad for an older man, but he doesn't have anything on me or any of my men.

He does everything with the worst holier-than-thou attitude I've ever witnessed, even from India. He's always judging everyone he encounters with those empty blue eyes. It's like staring into the calm of the deep depths of the ocean, knowing damn well a shark could take your arm off any second.

You'd think he was the king of our people with the air he presents himself with. He thinks that highly of himself, but luckily, as far as titles go, he's a nobody, and he knows it. Because I've made sure to remind him every couple decades, when the need arises. The only titles he's acquired are Commander's Father, King's Advisor's Best Friend, Lousy Father, Worthless Mate, and Asshole.

"It really is time you hired better help, son. That woman you have here tried to get an attitude with me and prevent my entry," he complains.

Remind me to give Matilda a raise and some flowers. Benny chuckles back in my mind as the guys enter the dining room.

"Hey, old man!" Benny bellows, clapping both of his hands on my dad's shoulders because he knows how much he hates it, not to mention how much I love it.

"Benjamin, I'll remind you that I do not answer to that title, and you can keep your hands to yourself."

The twins are already snickering, and I allow myself to think for a moment that maybe this evening may not be all bad. Sure, my father will do everything in his power to piss me off, and he will succeed, but I have my men. My brothers. They'll have him far more irritated by the end of dinner, and I'll get to enjoy the show.

Smirking at the thought, I head into the kitchen to confront India about the evening's new development. I'm barely through the door when her back runs into my chest, as though she were about to shove through the door with a breadbasket in her hand. "Playing chef and homemaker won't win you points with me when you just so happen to forget to mention that my father would be at dinner tonight."

She freezes for a single moment before regaining her composure. "He made me promise not to tell you he was coming. He wanted to surprise you," she says with a pout. I wish I could believe her, but she knows how much I loathe my father's presence. *What are they up to?* She shimmies past me in a hurry, leaving me in the kitchen with a moment to myself when I notice it actually smells kind of good in here. If the evening somehow doesn't turn into the shitshow I'm expecting, I'm going to try to remember to thank her.

"Oh, good evening, Avram; I didn't know you'd made it already!" she squeals with that shrill ring she gets in her voice when she's putting on a show, like when she's recording something for her followers.

Maybe the boys will take turns pissing her off alongside my father. *This might not be such a bad evening after all.*

Smirking, I head back into the dining room to find my father has taken Benny's seat at the other end of my table. I always sit at the head of the table, while Benny takes the other end. I guess I should be surprised that he didn't take my seat. Hell, maybe he thought he had. *It's okay, Boss, you know I don't give a shit about a chair. Let's just get through the meal so he'll leave.* Benny rationalizes in my mind. He's not wrong.

I dip my chin in a nod as I look at him, then the rest of my men, before taking my place at the table.

The men begin to take their seats after I've sat down, while India looks around frantically, trying to decide whether to sit by my side or my father's. She can have him for all I care, but I know I won't get that lucky. Like I said, he's a nobody, and that wouldn't be enough for the advisor's daughter. It almost makes me regret being in command of Zabella's armies. It's my reputation and strength that put me in this position. Add in my professional hockey career, and I'm just well and truly fucked.

"So, Father, what brings you through the rift gate and across the globe for dinner?" I ask, knowing it can't be good.

My hope drops even further when he smiles like that. He's proud of whatever he's about to say, while I will likely loathe the words that come from his mouth. "I have word from Boian," he says smoothly, all too happy with himself. Boian is the werewolf king's advisor, and India's father. My father latched on to him when they were young. Always striving for more than he was born with and never quite reaching it until he was able to use me.

My men know the direction this conversation is about to take and how I'll feel about it. They all visibly tense at his words. *At ease, men, don't react. He finds power in it.*

"Father, do you care to finish your sentence, or are you practicing the art of suspense?" I ask, feigning indifference, as I straighten my silverware next to my place setting.

I've obviously ruffled his feathers, judging by the small scrunch of his brows for only a moment, and I love it. "Well, son, it is most excellent news!" he exclaims as he claps his hands.

Nothing good can come from him being this truly happy with himself.

"Boian has informed me that the union of you and India

will be so much more than your average arranged marriage . . ." he pauses once again, for dramatic effect, and I can feel my resolve to not strangle him weaken. My men are just as restless. My wolf is growling and pacing under my skin.

"When you've finished with your silly little hockey career, you will return to Zabella, and you will no longer be commander of the army."

I'm up and out of my chair in an instant, letting the roar loose from my throat. "What are you going on about? No more of this illustrious bullshit. You have only a moment to tell me what's going on before this is no longer a nice family dinner."

My father takes a moment to straighten his cufflinks, like he doesn't have a care in the world, but I can see the tic in his jaw that tells me how he feels about me interrupting him. "Well, son, if you would let me speak. Now, as I was saying, you will no longer be the commander of our armies."

Small growls erupt around the table.

"As you know, our poor princess was lost to us some time ago. Though the King and Queen continue to hold out hope that she will be found, Boian has been in discussion with them for some time. They have finally all agreed that should our princess not be found by the time you're finished with your little hockey games, you, my son, will take the throne as king, with India as your queen."

All the men begin yelling into my mind at once, causing me to throw up my walls.

"What did you just say?" I ask in a calm and deadly voice. "I didn't ask for this. What if I don't want this? It's not enough to marry her to make your old pal happy, but now I'm to lose all my freedom and become King?!"

India flinches from the level of my voice, but I can tell she's still immensely pleased with herself.

I couldn't imagine her as the Luna of my pack, and they want her to be the Queen Luna of our existence? This is the most ridiculous thing I've ever heard. "Alright, Father, joke's over. What did you really want to talk about?" I ask.

"Roman, I will not be spoken down to again, and I do not spin fairytales. You will be king, whether you like it or not. Enjoy playing your silly games, and when the time comes, you will be king." With that, he stands, throws his napkin from his lap onto his plate, and storms out of my home with India hot on his heels. I'm sure she has questions and more ass-kissing to do, but I can't be bothered to care right now.

Once we're alone, all of my men look to me with different expressions on their faces. Benny is a mixture of shock, awe, and trying not to laugh his ass off. Eris and Dolos seem to be rendered speechless, which I haven't witnessed in a long time. Slate looks like he's going to kill someone, but he always looks like that so it's hard to tell if he's affected. Andrei looks a little confused, and maybe a little lost in thoughts or memories.

"I don't know anything more than all of you. I didn't know this was coming," I state, quietly.

"I think you made that clear with your father, but that doesn't change the fact that it's happening," Slate replies, always the logical one but he's not done yet, "should we talk about this and make a plan of some kind? There are going to be a lot of moving parts we'll need to take care of."

I've always been immensely grateful for my men, but they never cease to amaze me with their loyalty to me. "Thank you, Slate, but that's not needed yet. I don't plan to retire from hockey any time soon, and I'm not thinking about this right now. Let's just finish eating, and for now, we can pretend this didn't happen." And so, we did.

As the last of my men make their way out, leaving just Benny and myself at the table, Benny looks at me without a hint of humor in his words, "What now, Boss?"

I drop my chin for a moment feeling my wolf fight a mixture of rage and pride under my skin. Looking back up, I scrub my hand up and down my face and let it settle on the back of my neck, "Benny . . . for once I don't really know."

7
Leera

Clothes are scattered all over our room and I'm not any closer to actually choosing something to wear on my assignment. I can't find the right balance of professional, chic, and fun. *Is that even what you wear for sports photojournalism?* Photographing animals was so much easier. Animals didn't judge what you were wearing while you took their pictures.

It's also so much easier to plan photos and interview topics in theory. The thought of actually having to show up in front of these people, who aren't just people, they're super famous, and kind of gorgeous men, who play hockey for a living and still remember to follow the plan I wrote . . . is terrifying. I never realized how attractive these men actually are. It really isn't fair to us regular mortals that they can walk around looking like that. What if words fail me and I can't even speak? What if I pick the wrong clothes and look like a total fool and they don't even want to talk to me?

I flop, face first, onto my bed with a dramatic half sigh, half growl. I'm talking full blown Disney princess temper tantrum and scream into my pillow.

"Will you just ask me for help for once?" Zoey snickers from where she has her nose in a book, tucked comfortably into her bed. It's not that I don't want to ask for help; I just don't understand when it's okay to ask or at what point I become a nuisance.

With my face still in my pillow, I grumble, "Will you please help me? I don't know what to wear for my interview." She flies off the bed so fast that it makes me giggle. "If you wanted to help so much, why couldn't you butt in sooner?"

"You need to know you can ask for help, but it's been killing me!" she says with a wide smile on her face. "Plus, you're so pretty, I've been waiting for the chance to dress you up!"

"Oh . . ." I say with a blush spreading to my cheeks. I felt pretty to myself, but other than my parents, no one has ever directly called me pretty before, let alone *so pretty*. "Thanks, Zo," I mumble as she starts pinging around the room, gathering what she needs to put me together.

I'm so glad I let Zoey talk me into going shopping, so we had clothes for any occasion. My wardrobe has mostly, only ever, consisted of comfy pajamas, jeans, t-shirts, and leggings. Now, I have some mix-and-match suits, cuter casual clothes, and even some cute dressy clothes, should the need arise.

She's got things from both of our collections of clothes and accessories to put together an absolute knockout outfit. We're roughly the same size, so it's nice that we can share stuff. She's gathered my high-waisted, classic black pencil skirt, a soft-pink tank top with lace detailing across the neckline, a cropped, black blazer with giant rhinestones for buttons, and my silver pointed toe pumps. Luckily, most of the arena isn't as cold as the actual rink, so I think this will be a good balance.

How does she know me so well already? If my brain were fully functioning, this would be the exact outfit I would have chosen for myself. I'm short, like really short, so the pencil skirt hits just below my knees but hugs my curves perfectly.

Mom taught me a long time ago that women were built to have curves and never to strive for anything less than happiness and health. I had asked once if women were supposed to be as skinny as the ones you see in magazines and in the movies. I'd found I was still fuller than a lot of girls my own age if I'd see them out and about on our travels, but my mom loved me and taught me to love myself. All women are beautiful in their own way, and as long as they're happy and healthy, that's all that really matters.

After I've adorned all the items in the outfit, I add my mom's pearl necklace and my favorite moonstone ring. I stop in front of the mirror one more time to give myself the final once-over, and I'm happy with the final result. It feels like one of those movie moments where you almost don't recognize yourself. I've tied my long silver hair into a sleek, professional ballet bun. I went with a very natural make-up look and a light-pink matte lipstick.

"You could be business Barbie!" Zoey giggles as she flops back onto her bed, picking up the book she had discarded on her mission to dress me.

I'm still not sure I'm ready for this, but if I don't leave now, I won't be early, and being on time feels like being late.

How did people get anywhere before GPS apps? I think to

myself as I pull into the parking lot of the giant complex that they built for the Mogadore Predators' hockey team. I researched ahead of time and was impressed by the number of things the organization and players do here for the community. They have hockey leagues for all ages, and a few of the players even pop in to help coach sometimes. Lots of ice-skating opportunities and parties just for fun!

I pull into visitor parking, dig my press badge out of my purse, and pull it over my head. My first official assignment for my photojournalism career. I snap a quick selfie before taking one more deep breath and ambling out of the car with all my things.

I especially wanted to be early so I could snap some action shots of the team practicing before it was time to do the posed pictures and interviews. I never had much of an affinity for posed shots. It takes the subject out of their normal habitat, and you lose some of the magic; another reason animals are better than people.

Smiling to myself, I push through the large glass doors of the stadium, and I am overwhelmed by the smells and sounds everywhere. I walk up to the front desk and let the receptionist know I'm here. I flash her my press badge like they do in the movies and hope I don't look as nervous as I feel. She points me to the rink where the guys are practicing today. I nod with a small thank you and push myself through yet another set of doors and try to pull myself together.

In my research, I saw lots of pictures and watched a ton of video clips of the team playing, but standing here and seeing it with my own eyes is something else entirely. They're big, burly men but they move with just as much grace and agility as dancers we saw in a Broadway musical the time my parents had a piece to do about Central Park. Instead of music and bright colors, it's the scraping of their skates on the ice, the sticks, and the puck. Colors blur together and the breeze ripping from the rink as they go by feels like I've been transported to a whole other world.

When I'm able to shake myself from the weird spell and remember why I'm here, I bring my mom's camera to my face and snap a couple of shots. One of the goalie—what was his name again, oh yeah, Rau, Slate Rau—blocking a shot from going between his legs. The way his knees hit the ice and lock together to form a wall looks painful, but it's effective.

Another shot I got, that I think will turn out great, is one of the head coach hollering at the men while they run the drills. I finish off my covert photoshoot with a team shot after practice where the head coach stands in the center of the ice, all the men kneeling, and looking up to him while he speaks, their breath coming out in harsh plumes of air in front of their faces.

The older man claps his hands and yells at the men, "Hit the showers boys and make it fast, the student journalist will be here soon, and you better be on your best behaviors!"

As the last of them men shuffle through the locker room doors and out of sight, I make myself known, "Um, hi, good afternoon. I'm from Professor Sinclair's Photojournalism class."

"Ah! Hello there young lady! The guys are going to get cleaned up. Trust me, you do not want to have to smell them right now. We can start with my interview. Let's head to my office, then I'll get you set up with the guys. We can take your little pictures after all the interviews, if that works for you," he says as he starts walking.

I nod and trail a few steps behind him as I say, "Thank you sir, this is my first assignment so I'm a little nervous."

He chuckles with his gruff old voice.

I wonder if it's naturally gruff like that or if it's from years of yelling at hockey players. I think to myself with a small giggle.

"No need for all that sir nonsense young lady, you can just call me Coach."

"Thank you, Coach. I'm Leera, Leera Adams."

My interview with Coach went well. He answered all my questions and even told me a few stories about the guys. I asked him to go about his normal routine, and I snapped some pictures of him in his office environment. He also gave me a heads up about the starting players on the team, which is who I'll be interviewing today.

The goalie, Slate Rau, and the right wing, Andrei Roko, are quiet, and no matter what I say or do, they will likely not look happy or smile, but they'll be respectful and answer all my questions.

Eris and Dolos Marzzoli are twin brothers and are the starting defensemen. They'll be the easiest to talk to, as their nature is easy-going. They can also be ornery and overwhelming at times, though, so be aware.

Benjamin "Benny" Bucur is the left wing and back-up team captain. He'll also be easy to talk to, but I assumed as much from all my research. He handles himself well in post-game interviews and seems to radiate sunshine when he smiles.

Finally, there's Roman Razboinic, the center and team captain. All the men on the team are unjustly beautiful, but this man is otherworldly. He's huge, most athletes are, but come on! He's six foot six. That means he's literally twenty inches taller than me without my heels. He has naturally sandy-blondish-brown hair, a square jaw, and his nose is a bit crooked, probably from hockey.

That's not where my eyes got stuck in my research, though. Aside from being built like a semi-truck, he has heterochromia. One green eye and one blue. I couldn't find one picture of him smiling, and yet he remains the most gorgeous man I've ever seen. Just looking at him makes my heart beat funny. I've never been physically attracted to a man, but there's definitely a strange draw to him. He's also exceptionally intimidating, so I hope I won't have to interview him alone.

"Thank you for everything, Coach. This is perfect. Do you think it would be okay if we handled this in a group interview environment? I'd like to see how they all communicate with each other and really get the team vibe," I ask.

"If you think you can handle them all at once, they're all yours." He chuckles, and he's probably right. There won't be an easy way to do this.

He taps a button on his phone and says, "Julia, please let our starting six know that the interview will begin in ten minutes in the Blizzard party room."

Smiling to myself and gathering my things, Coach comes around his desk and holds the door open for me. "Thank you," I say lightly.

He nods and walks me down the hall, up a flight of stairs, and Into a party room overlooking the ice rink.

"These are usually used for birthday parties, but I thought

it would be better than the locker room with all their rank-ass gym bags."

I giggle another small thank you as I begin setting my things back up.

Only a few minutes later, Benny comes into the room with that sunshine smile of his, which is also so much better in real life. *I bet he gives the best hugs.* That was random.

"Hello, Mr. Bucur, my name is Leera," I say as strongly as I can while extending my arm for a handshake, hoping he can't tell how nervous I am.

His large hand swallows mine as he replies, "Hello, Leera, nice to meet you. Please call me Benny. Mr. Bucur was my grandfather. In fact, go ahead and call us all by our first names. None of us answer to our last names off the ice. The rest of the guys are on their way. Andrei and the boss will be a little late, and they told us to go ahead and get started."

Nodding my head, I turn back to my resources. *Roman must be the boss.* As I turn back around, Slate takes a seat in the back corner of the room. "Hi Slate, I'm Leera. Thank you for making time for me today," I say in my nicest voice, hoping not to upset the hulking giant of a man.

I'm still setting up a few things when the twins stumble into the room, shoving each other through the doorway. "Coach warned me about you two. Which one of you is which? I'm sorry if that's rude, but I can't tell, and I'd rather be sure."

They give each other a look that says they're thinking those ornery thoughts Coach warned me about, but I'm saved when Benny sets one on each side of the room. "This one is Eris," he says as he sets him on the right side, "and this one is Dolos," he says as he shoves him to the left. He then sits between them, and

I try to convey my thanks with a small smile.

Half an hour into the interview, everything is going great when the most curious sensation washes over me. It renders me speechless and a little lightheaded. "Are you okay?" Benny asks, immediately noticing my discomfort. It almost felt like that initial wave of anxiety when you know it's about to be a long day, but this is different. It's soft and warm, and I'm not sure how I feel about it.

I hear the doorknob, and my breath hitches in my chest when Roman walks through the door. The smell of cherry and leather washes over me, calming my nerves, but I can't breathe. Not like panic-attack-can't-breathe. It's different. When I'm finally able to gulp down some oxygen, I notice the room has gone unnaturally still, just as Roman's knees hit the floor.

8
ROMAN

Andrei and I finally finished up a meeting with one of the coaches for the youth league to iron out how and when the team can help, and we're headed to one of the party rooms to do this interview for some college kid's assignment. I usually don't mind this stuff, but I'm just really not in the mood. Frankly, I've been in a bad mood ever since my father dropped the king's bomb on me at dinner the other evening.

Just as we're about to walk through the door, I stop and take a step back. My wolf is whining and pacing relentlessly. I can't tell if something is wrong or if it's anticipatory. He feels like he very much wants what's on the other side of that door. Andrei's wolf seems to be having his own feelings because, as I look over, he looks like he's seen a ghost. His skin is white, and he's sweating. *What the fuck is going on?*

I open the door, but I don't make it two steps past the door frame when the world stops and the room starts spinning. My knees hit the concrete floors, and I can't breathe. There's a scream building in the back of my throat.

This can't be happening.

This isn't possible.

I'm struggling to catch my breath.

Am I dreaming?

Did I pass out and fall into a nightmare?

Benny looks between a gorgeous young woman at the front of the room and me with concern etched into his features, noticing we're both in some state of distress.

Mate. My wolf cries beneath my skin.

That's not possible. We already had a mate, and we lost her. I wasn't thinking, and my walls were still down. Benny's eyes take on the size of hockey pucks while he lowers himself into his seat, feeling the grief radiating from my body.

"What is this?!" I roar, causing the poor girl to flinch. This in turn causes my wolf to snarl viciously, as he has decided to have some form of attachment to this small human. I'm not able to calm down as the room remains silent and no one responds to me. All you can hear is heavy breathing from myself, maybe her, and a few of my men.

"I said, what is this?! Is this some kind of fucking joke?!" I continue to roar as I level the twins with a glare, noticing another flinch from the girl.

Slate rises from his seat, also looking concerned, when he nears me, where I'm still kneeling on the floor. I still can't breathe. I'm trying to gulp down oxygen, but my brain isn't listening, and my lungs feel like they're full of concrete. My wolf is raging now. The small woman in the center of the room is trembling, but she still doesn't look away from me.

Alpha, what's going on? Slate asks.

If it's what I think it is—Benny begins, but I cut him off.

My wolf thinks she's my mate. I feel it—the mate bond. I finish, shaking my head. *This can't be happening.*

All eyes in the room snap to my face. They all know my history. They all know about Imogen. About everything. They all know that she was all the good things in this world and in me. They know that I couldn't protect her. They know she was murdered. They know we never found out why she was killed. They know we never found her murderers. They all know I failed her. They all know I failed my only child. They all know this isn't possible. You only get one mate. *Right?*

Then why does this human also smell of spun sugar, honeysuckles, and sunshine, just like Imogen? It's all too much, and my eyes fill with tears. There are only two women who were able to bring tears to my eyes: my mother and my mate.

I'm able to pull myself up onto my shaky feet. "I don't know what kind of game is being played, but whoever is responsible for this will regret it," I growl. With that I slam the door on my way out of the room without looking back.

I'm halfway through the building when my mind registers the pained look on her face when I stormed out of there. I don't even know her name. *Who could have done something like this?* I haven't pissed off any witches in a long time, and I'm not sure even they have magic powerful enough to replicate a mate bond. My heart is aching both from the look on her face, and my wolf's declaration.

Brutus, I need an elder now! Not over mind link. Here. Now.

9

Leera

My body is still frozen in place when he slams the door, leaving me frightened, but I also immediately feel the loss of his presence in a way I don't understand.

The slamming door seems to break the spell my body was under, only I'm not prepared. Benny catches me before I hit the ground. I didn't even register that my legs were no longer supporting my body.

I just sit there in a crumbled mess when the trembling begins. This trembling is also different than anxiety where I get all cold and clammy. I'm warm, and thankfully, not sweating, but I feel all wrong. A small sob slips through my lips and every man in the room flinches. *That was weird.*

"Leera, can you stand? Let me get you in a chair," Benny says softly. Who knew this big hulking man could be gentle. I've watched clips of their games; they're savage on the ice.

I rise onto unsteady legs, but I'm able to hold my own weight. Instead of sitting in the seat with these men, I rush over to my things and begin to hastily pack everything up. This is not how this was supposed to go. Of all the possible things that I thought could go wrong, having a strange reaction to the team captain and pissing him off without muttering a word was NOT on that list. *Maybe I'm just getting sick. It has nothing to do with that man. Yea, that's it.*

"Hey, it's ok, you don't have to go," Benny nearly pleads.

Drawing my eyebrows together, "I'm sorry but did you just see the same thing I did? I don't know what you guys did to get on his nerves, but you didn't have to make me the punchline. This was just a class assignment I was trying to get done." I'm gasping and ranting and on the verge of a full-blown panic attack, but I don't have time for this. I have to get out of here.

I've thrown my things into my bag without even putting them in their folders. I'll deal with that later I have to get out of here. Benny is still trying to convince me to stay when I barrel out the room and move as fast as I can in this damn skirt. Why does photojournalism have to be such a broad spectrum? None of the wild animals we encountered were even a fraction as terrifying as that monster of a man.

But why did he look at me like that? He looked like he was having a similar reaction to me, but whereas mine was shock and attraction, his seemed to turn to anger and pain. *What could I have done to him to garner that type of reaction?*

I'm still shaken up as I barge through our dorm's door, effectively scaring the shit out of Zoey. "Whoa, whoa, whoa, what's wrong?" she asks, flying from her bed.

Using my arms far too much as I speak, I recount the entire moment since she saw me last, dropping onto the bed dramatically as I say the last word. I'm fiddling with my fingers, staring at my lap waiting for something, anything. I slowly peek up and Zoey's mouth is so wide open it looks like when someone dies screaming in those scary movies. Snapping my fingers in front of her face, "Earth to Zoey, come in Zoey!" She slowly closes her mouth and stares for another moment before breathing out a small, "Whoa . . ."

"I just tell you the weirdest, craziest, and scariest moment of my life, and all I get is *whoa*?" I stand and start pacing the room. "Oh my god my assignment! What am I going to do with my assignment? Just turn in some pictures and the interview with Coach?" I'm screeching now, and the panic is still climbing higher.

"Okay, okay, okay, this will be okay. Let's just think about this." Zoey says calmly. That's almost scarier than what I just went through, well that's a lie, but seriously, she's never the calm one.

I stop and take a deep breath, hold it for five seconds, and release it. *This will be okay.* There may not be a logical explanation for what happened, but I can use my logic to find a solution.

"Thank you, Zoey. You're right. This will be okay," I say as I grab my bag off the floor by the door. "First things first, I need to go through my stuff, see what I have, and decide what my next step is."

When I've sorted through all my papers and straightened out the ones that were slightly abused by my frantic escape, I decide that I have enough to turn in a pretty decent interview with Coach. Especially with that shot from the end of practice. "I've got it! I'll pitch it to Sinclair like this was the plan. Like the pre-season interview was set to focus on Coach while I follow up with the team just before the season!" Since Zoey has been listening to me rant and move about the dorm for the last hour, she just nods here and there.

"I can use my press badge and I'll . . . where's my press badge?" I begin to rummage through my bag, but I already went through it all. "Dammit! On top of everything I've lost my press badge?!" It was my turn to roar. *Can't something just go right today?!*

Realizing I've done all I can today, I accept defeat, and choose to figure it all out tomorrow. I grab my vitamins off my shelf and take them when I remember I'm nearly out of my doomsday stash my dad bought for me.

"Hey Zoey, do you know what kind of vitamins these are? I've looked everywhere and can't figure out which brand they are."

She takes the bottle and looks at the capsules, then shakes her head. "No, sorry. We never took vitamins, so I'm no help, but they just look like your standard multivitamin. Any brand should do."

I nod because that all makes sense. *Why was I making such a big deal about something so simple?* "Thanks Zo. I'm just gonna hop in the shower."

I let the hot water run over my body and try to sort through my thoughts. I might have gotten my papers sorted out and organized, but my mind is still a shitstorm.

Roman had terrified me, but my physical reaction to him was something I'd never experienced. I wasn't sure I ever wanted to experience it again. But another part of me definitely did, without a second thought. I had to find a way to see him again. Even if it's just to apologize for whatever that was, even though

I'm still kind of terrified of him, I have to know if my reaction was to him or some weird episode completely unrelated to the strange encounter.

While I finished my shower, I planned to present my idea to Professor Sinclair. I'll write up an amazing piece about Coach with the photos I snagged and propose a part two the day of the first game. What could be more hyped up than the first game of the season? Not only would it be the first game of the season, but news articles said it's against their number one rivals, the Augusta Vultures.

10
ROMAN

Four hours have passed since I stormed out of that party room, and I still can't get the look on her face out of my mind. The look on her face caused by my actions, by slamming the door and walking away. The look on her face because I left her. She didn't seem to understand the situation, and yet she still looked pained at my implied rejection. I didn't even speak to her. I don't even know her name.

I've demanded my men not speak her name. She was in such a hurry to leave, she managed to leave her press pass with her information on it behind, and Benny is hanging on to that at the moment. I don't want to know anything until I hear from the Elder. Benny did let me know that he tried to make sure she was okay before she panicked and ran away from them. *Where did she go? Is she okay?* My wolf is furious with me.

The Elder will be arriving any moment. She's one of the members that I had gone out of my way to find and bring back to the pack. No matter how much someone thought they knew, they never knew as much as the elder wolves who had lived through multiple millennia. This would be the first time I had to call on her in an official capacity.

As Matilda scurries past my doorway to open the front door, a small smile stretches across my face. I have a very soft spot for my little housekeeper. She's been with me for so long now I would do anything to make sure she was happy. So while my wolf and I are in turmoil over this situation, having an excuse to bring her sister to visit is just a bonus. They don't get to see each other as much since Matilda asked to join us in the city.

When I found Meredith, our eldest elder, she only promised to join our pack if I would bring her little sister with us. They'd always been together. Neither had found their fated mate or selected a chosen mate to have a family with. It's always just been the two of them, and who was I to separate them for selfish reasons when they could easily both come with us? It was an especially easy decision because, where Benny seemed to radiate sunshine, these two radiated kindness. They were the quintessential little old ladies, and everyone loved them.

Remembering why Meredith was here quickly pulled me from my happy thoughts, and the darkness resettled over me. I rose from my desk with a long sigh and made my way to greet her. "Thank you for arriving so quickly, Elder. I didn't know what to do," I say as I approach with my hand prepared for a handshake.

While the sisters might radiate kindness, they're still feisty and fiery in their old age. Meredith knocks my hand away while tsking and crooks her finger at me to come closer. Just as I move in and lean down enough for her to reach me, she wraps her arms around my shoulders and pats me on the back. Her hugs feel like hope, and I'm thankful she always insists everyone needs hugs.

She pulls away from me without releasing my shoulders and pushes my face back, assessing. "You're far too stressed. All those wrinkles. You're going to look older than me soon if you don't learn to lighten up," she chides in that sweet little voice of hers. "Come tell me what has you so bothered that you needed to speak in person."

"This is going to sound crazy, but . . ." I trail off for a moment, reliving all my emotions from mere hours ago. Feeling the mate bond that isn't possible, like I could somehow be happy again, but also the searing pain of what it felt like to lose Imogen; to feel like such a failure that I couldn't protect my mate and child. I allow the emotions to wash over me as I say, "Is there a way for someone to replicate, or manufacture, a mate bond? The feelings of finding your mate?"

I can tell she's intrigued because one of her eyebrows rises slightly while I speak.

"No, Alpha. While witches and other beings can do much with their powers, the mate bond is a sacred bond given to us by the Moon Goddess herself. I have never heard of such a thing." I think she's done talking when she continues, "But . . . it is exceptionally rare. I've only heard of it happening twice in all of werewolf history," she says as she wrings her hands together, lost in thought.

"Elder Meredith, can you please tell me what you're thinking?" I was trying not to lose my patience, but that rope was fraying fast.

"Let's sit," she says, taking my hand and leading me to the sofa in the living room. I feel like a small boy in trouble and waiting to learn his punishment with her leading me this way, but I'm too focused on what it is she could have to say.

She sits first and pats the seat for me to join her. I do as she requests, waiting for her to speak. When she doesn't begin, I look over to find her still lost in thought.

"What's going on?" I finally ask as my patience wears thin.

"Alpha, I believe you've been given a second chance. Because we are immortal, when we pass, our souls usually join the Goddess until the pair is ready to find each other in the next life cycle. There have been a few occasions where a mate's soul was returned to the same life cycle to live another life with their mate. We do not know why this happens or what the Goddess uses to determine when and why someone should get their mate back. It looks like the Goddess favors you, young man. You better not take this blessing for granted."

"What?"

Of all the things she could have said, I was not expecting this. *Could it be true? Am I being given a second chance? But why? What have I done to earn the Goddess's blessing?* "How can this be? Are you truly saying that Imogen's soul is the same soul now residing in that young woman?"

She nods with a small smile on her face when she says, "I didn't get to meet your Imogen, and I haven't met this young woman, but your wolf knows your mate's soul. If he identified her as your mate, then you should trust him."

Men, join the Elder and me in the living room; we have news that I was not expecting.

They come pouring into the room as if they were waiting just outside the threshold. Judging by the looks on the twins' faces, that's exactly what they were doing.

Crossing my arms across my chest, I say, "You already heard

everything, didn't you?" Benny is the only one who has the decency to look almost abashed by being caught snooping.

"She's really your mate, isn't she? How can this be?" Andrei speaks up. He's also been a little off-kilter since that little woman threw my world into disarray.

Mate. My wolf seems to release the tension of not understanding what is happening. I can feel the support radiating from my men, and I send a silent thanks to the Goddess not only for giving me another chance with my mate but for these men who have become my family.

"Yes, she is my mate, and therefore, your Luna." As the words leave my mouth, I realize I have more questions.

"Meredith, has a reincarnated mate ever been human? I didn't sense a wolf or other supernatural energy from her."

She doesn't immediately respond, tapping her chin in thought, "No, I don't believe so, but the Goddess does all with a purpose. What is meant to be will be."

Nodding to myself, my thoughts wandered again to the look on her face as I left her standing there alone and confused. "Thank you, Elder Meredith. You may stay and spend time with your sister for as long as you like. I'll have her make up a spare room for you."

"Thank you, Alpha; that sounds wonderful. I may extend my stay a while to also meet our new Luna." My only reply is a small nod as I walk towards my office.

Benny, you're with me. He'll catch you all up afterwards.

Plopping into my chair, I rub my hands all over my face, and through my hair, trying to absorb the colossal information overload I'm enduring while simultaneously trying to think ahead.

Benny comes through the door moments later looking plenty disheveled himself, "I can't believe this is happening. Are you sure you don't want to know her name now?" he asks as he pulls the press pass from his pocket, dangling it in front of me like a dog with a bone.

"Yes, I'm sure. The first time I hear her name, I want to hear it from her voice. I haven't even heard her speak. I can't believe she's so young. Which school is she attending?" He turns over the press pass and shows me the Mogadore State Warriors logo on the back. "I'll need to call and let the professor know something came up and we can make up the interview after our first game."

Benny is just smiling and nodding now, until his face falls, "Uh, Boss . . . I hate to be the one who bursts your bubble, but what are you going to do about India and the King?"

SONOFABITCH! How could I forget about the mess that the rest of my life is? "For now, we do nothing. I don't want India or my father to know anything about her until I know everything, and she accepts the bond if this is really happening."

I don't know what's going to happen with her being a human. None of our pack members have been fated to a human but we know it can happen. The bond isn't as strong for humans and rejecting it doesn't nearly kill them as it does with us.

"Tomorrow I'll make the calls to make this right and meet the new life of my mate."

11

Leera

After strategizing my outfit with Zoey again, I march into my Photojournalism class ten minutes early to speak with Professor Sinclair.

I take a moment just outside the door to give myself a quick pep talk before assuming my confident posture and walking into the room.

"Ah Leera! Perfect, perfect, I was hoping for a moment to speak with you," she exclaimed before I could even take in a breath.

"Good morning, Professor. I wanted to talk to you about my assignment with the Predators if you have a moment."

"No need dear, Mr. Razboinic already called to let me know," she says airily like there's really no way she knows how that day really went. "He did?" I asked with a small squeak in my voice.

"Yes. He called to apologize for having to miss the interview with the group. He was asking if you could use your interview with the coach and follow up with an assignment for their opening game this week."

On one hand, he took care of all of this for me, but on the other, WHAT THE HELL?

Just as I'm about to ask more, she shoves a brand-new press pass across her desk as students start to trickle into class. "If you have any other questions, let's discuss them after class," she says quietly as she shoots me a wink.

I had a speech planned out and everything. *So maybe he doesn't hate me?* If he hated me, he would have blamed the interview disaster on me and not invited me back.

With it being such a big game, I did some additional research on the Vultures. Their team captain is Khaos Mokotoff. Apparently, he and Roman always fight hard during their games. This will be huge for my classes and me. Can you imagine how intense this game will be? Maybe I can keep working with the team if I can ace this article.

What if my body freaks out around him again, though? I need to be prepared for whatever that was. I've seen plenty of attractive men around the world, and sure, they're nice to look at, but my body has never felt like *that* before.

It was like something deep inside of me decided I wanted him without my brain's consent. But it also kind of felt like a weird panic attack. It can't be normal, though, can it? I know I'm obnoxiously incompetent when it comes to matters of attraction, having never even kissed a boy or felt compelled to . . . you know . . . pleasure myself. I mean, I've tried a couple times, but I didn't know what I was doing, and I don't think I did it right. Jeez, I must be fifteen shades of red right now. Maybe I could talk to Zoey about this stuff. Gosh, it's so embarrassing, though.

Class flies by while I try to focus on what's actually being taught, but my mind continues to drift back to a certain hockey player with sandy hair and what he might look like if he smiled. I hope he's in a much better mood next time. I check my press badge for the game information, but it doesn't say if the interview is before or after the game, and I'm not sure if there's a standard protocol for these things.

When class is finally over, I take my time gathering my things. One other student waits to talk to the professor, so I patiently wait my turn. "Hey Leera, did you need anything from me?" she asks as I approach her desk.

"No, thank you. I mean, yes. I mean, I don't need anything; I just have a quick question. Do you know if the interview is before or after the game or anything?"

"I believe my understanding was that after the game, you can participate in the postgame press conference for your interview," she responds.

"Oh, okay, that makes sense. Thank you, Professor."

I spent the next two days perfecting my interview questions. I have a set of questions for if they win and a set of questions for if they lose. I like to be prepared for either outcome, but since it's a trait I got from my father, my need for organization and order has only increased since his passing. My therapist promised that it was just a way for me to manifest my grief and that as long as I didn't let the tendencies completely impact my life, I would be okay.

Everything I need for my interview tomorrow is packed up in my new, chic little briefcase I bought myself to feel more professional. With my father still on my mind, I go to take my vitamins. I only have one left from the stockpile he had accumulated for me. A strange part of me doesn't want to let it go. I know it's a weird thing to be attached to, but since I couldn't find the same ones, I'm struggling with this.

I settle on keeping the last vitamin in the last bottle, and I put it back on my shelf. Cracking open a brand-new bottle of multivitamins that I picked up at the grocery store, I allow myself to remain positive and focus on another piece of my new beginning.

12
ROMAN

I t's the first game of the season and instead of being ready to destroy the Vultures, I'm distracted by the thought of a certain silver haired miracle. The men are wound up and shouting across the locker room at each other and I still can't get in the moment. I need to give my pre-game pep talk, but I'm just not here mentally. I can't sense her yet, and I don't know if the reason she chose not to come is because of our last encounter. Maybe she's just not here yet, or maybe it's because I'm stuck in this rank-ass locker room with a bunch of sweaty wolves.

Coach seems to sense my turmoil. He pats me on the shoulder, making his way to the center of the locker room. "All right, LISTEN UP!" he bellows. The men immediately quiet and turn their attention to the old wolf. "I thought with it being the first game of the season you wouldn't mind letting the old man give the pep talk today," he says as the men chuckle around the room.

His speech is motivating, empowering, invigorating, and most of all, it's got the men all pissed off and ready to slaughter the Vultures. I definitely couldn't have brought out those emotions today. I need to get my head in the game.

I made sure to set everything up so that she can be part of the postgame interview even though it's supposed to be for seasoned journalists. Little do they know I have another plan up my sleeve as well. I don't want her interview to suck, which is why I need to get my head on straight so we can beat them. Not that I'm worried about my team, but with Khaos being the Vulture's team captain . . . I really just can't afford a loss today for any reason.

The electric energy of the crowd as we skate onto the ice for our warm-ups is exactly what I needed. No matter how many games we play, I never take this feeling for granted. I wonder if this is how an incubus feels all the time, feeding off people's energies. It's no wonder the few I know are part of the music industry.

The stands are filling with people of all ages, sizes, and backgrounds all coming together to watch us play. The buzz of the arena continues to climb towards crescendo as more and more people file in. Everywhere you look, there are people smiling, laughing, scowling, and hollering as the teams take to the ice.

It's not enough that it's the first game of the season, but it's against the Vultures. That means this game is going to be intense. Probably a few brawls, maybe even a little blood. A lot of that has to do with Khaos and I, but our men despise each other equally. I don't know if Benny or the twins are more excited for what they hope will be a blood bath of a game.

We're warming up when she walks in. I can't find her in the madness of the arena, but I can feel her. I know she's here, and I let the warmth of the mate bond wash over me. I haven't felt this feeling in five hundred years, and I definitely never expected to feel it again. The initial shock still hasn't worn off, but now I know it's real; this is really happening. I have another chance. I don't know what I did, or will do, to deserve this, but I will make the most of every moment. I can never thank the Goddess enough for this precious gift.

It's the season opener, so the pregame show is even more loud and obnoxious than usual. The fans, human and not alike, go feral for it. The loud music, the flashing lights, and the T-shirt cannons are all pounding along with the beat of my heart. Usually, it's all game energy but tonight is different. Yes, it's the first game of the season, but she's here and she changes everything.

As my name is called to skate onto the ice with my men, I allow myself one more chance to look around the rink to see if I can spot her in the sea of faces. I'm not able to locate her , but I can feel her excitement through the bond, and for now that will have to be enough. I do manage to make eye contact with Khaos, so while I have his attention, I flip him off. The arena erupts again as he attempts to lunge at me, but his team holds him back.

The first period was mayhem. It didn't seem as though anyone even cared about the puck as much as they did just beating the shit out of each other. I spent the whole time avoiding getting pummeled, while still trying to find my girl. If I could just see her for a moment, maybe then I could focus on the game.

We're already into the second period, and Khaos and his men seem to sense my distraction. They've gotten a lot more shots in on me than usual. I haven't scored a single goal, but thanks to Slate, they haven't either.

13

Leera

Walking through the large doors of the hockey arena again caused a slight panic when I recall the only other time I was ever here. Panic isn't the only thing I feel, though. I don't know how, but I swear I can feel *him*. It's like this weird awareness and warmth. Like, my body knows he is here and wants to find him. *This is so weird. Am I excited to see him, or do I want to avoid him for as long as possible?* I think to myself.

I catch a glance of myself in the floor-to-ceiling glass walls and smile. Zoey has named herself not only my best friend but now also my fashion manager. She had a plan of action ready before I could even stress myself out with what to wear.

The Mogadore Predators' team colors are maroon, black, and white, which was awesome for me. The colors complement me perfectly.

Zoey had my clothes all laid out on display for me when I got home to get ready for the game. "Have I told you lately how much I love you?" I ask, taking in the outfit that was the perfect combination of warm, professional, and gorgeous.

"No, you haven't, but I'll take payment in the form of my own hunky hockey player. Put in a good word for me," she says with a wink.

Scoffing dramatically and rolling my eyes, I take in my ensemble for the evening. She's taken this job especially seriously, as she seems to think I'm much more experienced with men than I am.

It starts with the cutest black lace bra and panty set that I had sitting in the back of my drawer for this normal college girl experience I wanted to maybe have. The next layer consists of some black pleather leggings and a long-sleeve black T-shirt. There's a perfect maroon, oversized, chunky sweater to keep me warm in the arena. The finishing touches are a fluffy black infinity scarf and my warm black snow boots. To keep my hair from turning into an electric science experiment from the scarf, I pull it into the messiest, messy bun, pulling a few pieces loose around my face for that perfect look.

I felt so pretty when I looked in the mirror but I'm second guessing everything now. I was so confident in my outfit last time and look how that went. I sigh and shake my head at myself for allowing my thoughts to take that direction. I needed to channel more of Mom's whimsy nature, but it seemed to be evading me lately.

Chic little briefcase in hand, I straighten my spine, make my way inside and flash my press badge to the receptionist.

Warm-ups have already started, and I mentally scold myself for not getting here sooner. I've been studying as much hockey information as I can to understand what's going on tonight, and I wanted to be here for the full experience of watching the teams skate onto the ice and such.

Nevertheless, I make my way into the stands to find my seat. Luckily, I'm seated with a lot of other Predators' fans. I'm a couple rows up from the second-level railing, and I have a great view of the entire rink. In my research, I found that the Vultures and Predators have a lot of bad blood and are one of the league's biggest rivalries. The last thing I wanted to do today was get in the way of some crazy sports brawls by being stuck with fans from the wrong team.

The closer I got to the rink, the stronger the strange pull in my body became. The second I could see the ice, my body felt like it would lurch out there with all the players. With all their gear on, I couldn't tell which one he was until I saw the giant number twenty-three on his back. He seems to be looking for something in the stands. *I wonder if he's looking for me.* Just as the thought crosses my mind, his head turns toward me, and for some reason I choose that moment to hide behind a couple of guys in the row in front of me.

I still haven't decided if I'm excited to see him or afraid from our last encounter. I slowly peek back out of my hiding spot to watch as the pregame show begins, the starting players are announced, and the game begins.

You can immediately feel the tension in the entire arena. It's radiating from the ice; it's so thick that it feels like you could reach out and grab it. These two teams hate each other very much; that is clear. The power they use to slam each other into the walls, rattling the plexiglass protector that keeps us from being hit with wild pucks, is otherworldly. Not only the power, but they're also so incredibly fast that there have been multiple moments where I could barely keep track of the puck.

Each time Roman gets close to looking in my direction, I

chicken out and hide behind someone near me. He's probably not even looking for me; why would he? But I don't know . . . it just feels like he is. I'm small enough, so it's not a difficult task. I guess it's not really fair of me, though, since I'm sitting here totally engrossed in every move he makes. Trying to ignore all the strange feelings in my body is another situation entirely, and I'm failing miserably at pretending it's not happening.

14
ROMAN

Two periods into this game and I'm borderline feral. We have to win this game and it's the last period.

I still haven't been able to spot her.

I can feel her.

I know her general area, but my eyes haven't met hers and it's driving me mad.

I'll have to run all night to burn through this anger.

Not only have I not been able to spot her yet, but the appropriately named Vultures, have locked in on my distraction and have been pummeling the shit out of me.

Boss, it would be so fucking helpful if you could pull your head out of your ass. Benny growls in my mind, followed by the team's grunts of agreement.

I'm trying. My wolf and body refuse to give a fuck about the game.

All right, *look, if we can finish this game, and win it, we know we'll get to see her for the fucking interview. Could you fucking cooperate with me here,* I scold my wolf. Using all my energy to focus on the game, I nod my head at Benny.

We're immediately barreling down the ice to get the puck back. After slapping down a Vultures pass, I pass the puck to Benny as he skates along the boards then cuts the middle. He shoots the puck towards the net, but their goalie makes the save. But I'm waiting on the edge of the crease and manage to snatch the rebound out of the air with my stick, lifting the puck over the goalie's mitt and into the net.

The entire arena erupts into madness as the buzzer goes off at the same time the puck hits the back of the net.

Just as I throw my arms up in the air in celebration, I'm hit from behind. My entire body is thrown backwards as another body barrels through my knees from behind me, then taking my legs out from under me. As my body falls to the ice, Khaos is there using his body to propel mine down harder, making sure this is more than just a hockey hit.

My head hits the ice first.

The impact is so strong that my vision blurs.

I know I'm going to black out.

I feel it coming.

I haven't been hit this hard in a long time.

Just as I'm about to allow myself to be pulled into the darkness, my little mate flies from wherever she was sitting.

She moves so fast that her snacks scatter everywhere as she sprints down the few steps and leans against the railing, screaming my name.

Hearing my name leave her lips is everything.

I want to reach out to her.

I want to tell her it's going to be okay.

I want to apologize.

I want to know her name.

But the darkness is too strong, and the worry etched into her face is the last thing I see as I'm enveloped by nothingness.

15
Leera

I knew hockey was brutal, but this seems so much worse than the games and highlights I watched.

The whole game has been that way for every play—someone's starting a fight or slamming someone into the wall.

I swear I saw a tooth fly across the rink earlier.

The harder the teams fight, the louder the fans scream. I can't explain the energy, but it doesn't feel like just a sports game anymore. The rivalry feels toxic, like the players' anger is seeping into the fans and everyone is just one wrong play away from being rabid animals.

It's been really intense. Both teams are constantly putting all their energy into pulling their team ahead in hopes of winning the game.

I'm trying to keep up with the plays and the lingo all while watching every move Roman makes.

It goes on like this for nearly the entire game. It's the third and final period when all of a sudden he seems more focused. Out of nowhere, Benny and Roman are skating so fast and all

I can do is gawk. Then they've got the puck! Benny is about to score, but the Vulture's goalie blocks it.

Oh, wait! It happens so fast I almost miss it, Roman has the puck in the net!

I'm about to cheer when a scream barrels from my body before I can truly comprehend what's happening.

There's no other way to describe it, other than, Roman is attacked. One man takes out his legs while another pummels him into the ice so hard I swear I can feel his pain.

My scream morphs into a wail of his name as I hurl my body down the steps of the arena to the railing overlooking the ice.

He sees me. His eyes stare right into mine. "ROMAN!" I yell one more time with my hand stretched against the plexiglass barrier. A moment later he loses his battle with consciousness and his eyes close.

I'm banging on the plexiglass divider and yelling now.

There are more security guards coming for me than there are refs helping Roman! The Predators' players are all flying on to the ice, but why aren't they getting to him faster?

Why do I care so much?

Why is this hurting me?

It doesn't matter, this is wrong.

Security obviously thinks I'm some kind of crazy lady. They're escorting me out of the building while fans are on the verge of brawling themselves. This is a nightmare. *Is this really happening?*

I struggle against the security team, letting them know I'm here as a journalist and was invited by Roman, but they don't stop moving even when I show them my press pass. Before they've gotten me out the door, I catch a glimpse of Benny and the twins standing over Roman. I've never seen a picture of an angry Benny, but right now, standing over his best friend's body, he looks like a very, very dangerous man.

I realize I'm still crying as I walk into our dorm room and Zoey is instantly on high alert.

I called her on the way home and gave her an idea of what happened.

"Shhhh, it's okay, come here," she soothes. She really is good at this. "I thought you didn't like the big bad wolf," she barely gets out without giggling.

"This isn't funny, Zo. I can't explain it, and I don't know why I care. I've never even had a conversation with the man, but there's just SOMETHING . . ." I emphasize by running both hands down my face and pulling at my eyes, looking like a kid making scary faces.

"There are already videos of that hit online, I saw the whole thing. Everything looked so crazy tonight. Hockey is tough and all, but it's not usually that bad. I guess the league made a statement and the other guy just has a fine to pay."

I just shake my head, still trying to fully process what just happened.

"Did they say whether or not he was okay?" I plead.

"They said once he woke up, he went a little crazy but he's okay. That happens sometimes when people wake up from being knocked out like that. Um, also . . . there's a couple videos of you. All the captions and comments keep asking why the little mystery girl freaked out," Zoey informs me quietly.

"Uuughhhhh," I sigh, just leaving my head in my hands at this point. "I don't even know what came over me. It was like I wasn't in control of my body or reactions!"

"It's okay, girl. Sometimes you just feed off the energy in those situations."

I know she's trying to make me feel better, but it just doesn't.

"Whatever. I'm so over this day. Can we just forget today ever happened?" I ask going to get ready for bed and try again tomorrow. When life gets hard, which it seems to want to do a lot lately, I find myself just wanting to put a pin in everything and deal with it later. Later being whenever, if ever, I'm ready to unpack what I'm actually feeling. Feelings are hard and heavy, and after I lost my parents, I find myself not wanting to really deal with those feelings.

When I emerge from our bathroom, Zoey grimaces and tries to smile.

"So, I guess you'll have to ask for another extension on your assignment," she says so quietly I can barely hear her.

My head snaps around so fast, "I hadn't even thought of that yet! I can't believe on top of everything else, I let her down again."

I drop on to my bed, feeling absolutely drained. Zoey also crawls into bed, turns on the TV and asks, "Cinderella or Beauty and the Beast?"

"Beauty and the Beast, definitely."

We both fall asleep watching dishes dance across the screen. I don't know what Zoey dreams about, but I keep reliving that hit over and over again on a loop.

16
ROMAN

Coming back to consciousness to find Benny pacing around my bedroom still in his gear was unsettling to say the least. The twins were sitting in the corner, actually quiet for once, and I'd be lying if I said it wasn't slightly terrifying. Andrei and Slate were locked in some kind of conversation. *Was I really hit that hard? It looks like a wake in here.*

They haven't realized I'm awake, but the grunt that slips through my lips as I try to set myself up alerts them immediately.

"Hey, hey, hey, whoa there, Boss. You took a nasty hit, slow down." Benny worries as he nears me.

"I'm fine, Benny. Take your mother hen act somewhere else," I grumble still trying to sit up. He doesn't listen, of course. He just quietly comes to my side and helps to balance me.

I still don't understand how our fans think we're human. The only humans that learn of supernatural beings are usually fated mates and sworn to secrecy. It's not that we want to remain hidden, it's just how the world is. Humans are too easily upset by things they can't understand or control. A hit like that would have killed a human. Sure, I'm still a little out of it, but thanks to my werewolf healing I'll probably be fine in another hour or so.

Just as the thought crosses my mind, so does the last thing I saw. "My mate, she was there, she was upset, is she okay?"

They all look at their shoes, refusing to make eye contact as Andrei barely shakes his head. I throw myself into a standing position, swaying on my feet, "Where is she?! What's wrong?!"

Benny is there immediately to steady me, "Boss, slow down. She was so upset by the hit that she went a little crazy herself and mmmhmhmhmmm," he trails off with a mumble.

"Don't fuck with me BENJAMIN! WHAT. THE. FUCK. HAPPENED?"

So quietly I don't know if I'm hearing with my ears or through our mind link, Andrei says, "Security kicked her out of the arena."

"WHAT?! And you all did nothing?" I roar, throwing things off the table in the room, really wishing I could kill something.

"We didn't have that option! We were standing over YOUR limp body, but you don't remember that part. YOU are our responsibility. She was upset, and it killed us to see our Luna that way, but she'll be fine!" The strength in Benny's response catches me off guard. That's when I see it. He was scared. Scared for me. They all were.

Furiously scrubbing my hands over my face and through my hair, "Shit guys, I'm sorry. She's got me all fucked up and that hit didn't help. I'm fine. I'm sorry you had to worry like that. Is everyone else okay? Did we win the game?" I ask, feeling my anger dissipating as I look around the room at my men. My brothers. My family.

"Everyone else is fine, and yeah we won, whatever," Slate

sullenly responds.

"You went down hard, Boss. It was hard to see you down like that and have to watch them drag her out of the stands and then drag you off the ice . . . it was a lot," Benny adds.

"I'm okay. We'll get them back for this. Is there anything else?" I ask, trying to get my thoughts in order.

"Uh yeah, kinda . . . you're not gonna like it," Eris says quietly. He's never quiet.

This is probably bad. I'm probably going to freak the fuck out again. "Just spit it out, I don't have the patience for this shit."

"So, obviously the hit is all over the internet . . ." he says, trailing off again.

"Goddamn it. SPIT IT OUT."

"theygotheronvideoallupsettoo" Dolos mumbles.

Kneading my fingers in the center of my forehead, "What. Did. You. Say?"

"Your hit isn't the only video blowing up the internet, Boss," Benny chimes in, again not making eye contact but he's slowly extending his phone in my direction with a video up, ready to hit play.

Before hitting play, I narrow my eyes at him, taking his phone from him without breaking eye contact.

I turn my eyes to the phone and hit play. I was not prepared for what came next.

The video is not of me or the hit. The video is of my mate. My heart crashes around in my body as she screams, and I feel her cries deep in my soul. The look on her face. The tears streaming down her face. Her body being drug away by those idiot security guards. I already wanted to murder Khaos. Now I want to torture him and make him beg for death. I kind of want to murder the security guards for touching her, but they're just following orders. If the video wasn't bad enough, the bullshit comments about a crazy woman set my blood to boil.

Immediately directing all my attention to Slate, "Make these go away. She doesn't deserve to deal with this," I snarl, trying not to hurl Benny's phone back at him; I know this isn't their fault. "That's not all."

The way Benny lifts just one eyebrow always reminds me of Ace Ventura before he gets into trouble. Chuckling at his antics, I say, "I need to see my girl."

"Hell yeah, Boss. Let's go get her!" He's out of the room before I have time to ask more questions.

"The rest of you stay here; do damage control. I don't care about my image; take care of your Luna," I say, glancing around the room.

They each give me a short nod in return.

Grabbing some clean clothes, I head into the bathroom, connected to my bedroom, for a hot shower. I need to wash that game from my body before I see her again—really see her.

Turning the water on to warm up when a thought hits me, "DAMMIT," I roar out loud, realizing I didn't get to finish my surprise for her. I'll have to rearrange that for another game. Maybe it's better this way. I can surprise her after we've properly met and had the chance to get to know one another a bit.

Stepping into the scalding water, I tip my head back and sigh. My body feels almost completely healed, but my soul is sore for her and what she went through. My wolf is whining and snarling around like this is all my fault. *We're going to go see her. We're going to take care of her.*

That seems to calm him a bit, allowing me to finish washing

away any remnants of the game and the hit. I don't want our first official meeting to be tainted by anything. Just the thought of her perfect body and gorgeous face sends blood running straight to the wrong end of my body. It's not the time for this. I switch the water to ice-cold and give my body a moment to cool off.

Cooled enough, I dry myself and dress to meet her. The one person in the universe with the power to bring me to my knees, but just as the thought crosses my mind, Imogen's face flashes into view.

My heart crumbles, and for a moment, I worry that I can't handle this again. *What if something happens? What if it feels like betraying her?* But it's not like that. But if she's truly my mate, then they share the same soul. The Moon Goddess sent her back to me. Will she regain old memories? At the same time that I don't want that for her, what if she could tell me who took her from me the first time? Either way, souls aside, Imogen would want me to be happy. She would be hurt by the way I have lived for the last five hundred years. I'm ashamed that it took her reincarnation for me to come to this realization.

Packing those thoughts away for now, I focus on my mate. The little human with silver hair who has invaded my every thought since I met her. I have to see her. I have to hear her name come from her lips. I have to make her mine.

As I walk into the open living space of our home, Benny hops off the couch, also dressed in clean clothes.

"So, how do we find her?" I ask, realizing I should have thought of that before.

"Well, I can't show you because it has her name on it, but"—he puts his hand in his pocket, pulling out her press pass and dangling it in front of me—"I might have had Slate hack the university systems to get all her information, including her dorm, and brought a guardian from the pack to look over her." I can tell he's partially proud of himself and partially worried I'll be pissed. My initial reaction is to be pissed because he didn't tell me. But instead of reacting, I give it another moment of consideration and realize he did the right thing.

"Thank you, Benny. Let's go get my girl."

17
Leera

I'm startled awake by a knock on the door. Zoey is in her bed snoring, so it's not her.

Whoever it is knocks again, "I'm coming!" I whisper shout, "Will you please shut up? It's the middle of the night!"

Checking my watch for the time, it's not as late as I initially thought, though it's still after eleven o'clock. It feels later after the night I had, I guess.

I crack the door open, and all the air gets pulled straight from my lungs. My body is instantly on fire, and it feels like electricity is pinging off the walls. *WHAT IS THIS?!*

His large body seems to take up all the space in the narrow hallway. "R-roman," I stutter like an idiot before reality hits me. "Oh my god, how are you standing here? You were hit so hard! Are you okay?" I'm whisper-yelling again because I'm in shock but aware enough that I don't want to be the jerk that wakes her roommate and a whole dorm hall.

With all the thoughts bouncing around my head and coming out of my mouth I just now notice he hasn't even moved. *Is he breathing?* He's just staring at me looking torn. Somewhere between drowning in painful memories, but also like when an animal sees fresh meat.

That's when I realize I'm standing in front of him in my pajamas. Pajamas you don't even wear to run to Walmart. Pajamas you don't wear for your first real encounter with the man you can't get off your mind. They're my comfiest pajamas, but they only consist of silk white shorts and a cropped camisole.

"Oh my gosh, I'm so sorry. I was asleep when you knocked, and I wasn't thinking." I feel my whole body turn red with embarrassment as I spin around to grab my fluffy pink robe off the back of the door.

I notice a similarly embarrassed Benny elbow Roman a little as I cover myself up.

Roman is still just staring at me. He looks so out of place in my boring dorm hallway. I mean the man is the size of a truck! They both are. Then you add in the beauty of these two men, and no one stands a chance.

Roman is all hard edges where Benny seems smoother and more relaxed. Since he's staring, I decide to stare a little too. Starting with his sandy blonde-brown hair, forehead wrinkled in thought, and jeez, even his muscles have muscles. He's just wearing a pair of well-loved jeans and a white T-shirt that hugs all of those muscles, leaving little to the imagination. While all of him is gorgeous, my entire body goes on alert when I stare into his eyes. I've never seen more captivating eyes. Not even in all the creatures we photographed around the world. One is a shocking cerulean blue, while the other is as green as the first blades of grass in the spring.

I don't know how long we stand there just staring at each

other until Benny makes a small coughing sound.

I'm not sure whether it's from the intensity of his stare, or being caught staring myself, but it's all a little much, so I lower my head and begin to fidget when I ask, "Roman are you okay? What's going on? It's almost midnight."

A hand broaches my line of sight and I watch as it very slowly approaches my face. The moment he makes contact it feels like the world stops.

My body is no longer mine. There's a tingling where we're connected and it's the most amazing thing I've ever felt. *WHAT IS THIS?!* With his index finger curled under my chin, he slowly tips my face up so I'm staring into his eyes again. I swear my heart is going to stop, and that was before he started talking.

Oh lord, now he's smiling and it's even more beautiful than I ever could have imagined. Then he says in a low, gruff voice, "Can we take a walk and talk?"

For several moments words leave me, and I just nod a little until my ability to speak finally returns.

"Let me throw on some real clothes real quick and I can meet you out in front of the building. I don't want you to get in trouble for being in here . . . wait how DID you get in here?"

He just smiles like he knows it muddles my thoughts, takes my hand in his, kisses the top of my knuckles, and begins walking down the hallway as he tosses a smile over his shoulder.

How can a man make me feel like my heart is going to stop and beat out of my chest at the same time?!

I close the door softly, holding on to all the calm energy I can for a moment. Once the door is closed and I hear their heavy footsteps fade away, I whisper-screech as I rush across the room. "ZOEY!"

"WHAT, WHAT, WHAT?!" she cries sitting straight up in bed and removing her eye mask.

"ROMAN. Just. Knocked. On. Our. Door," I squeak out, thumb hooking over my shoulder in the direction of the door. I think I might be on the edge of hyperventilating.

Zoey is out of bed now, eyes the size of saucers, rubbing her hands up and down my arms. "Breathe Lee, it won't do you any good if you pass out. Remember, deep breath in. Hold it. 5. 4. 3. 2. 1. Release . . . better?"

I nod.

"Okay, let's try that again. What's going on?" she pries.

I take one more deep breath and get all my words out on the release of that same breath, "Roman and Benny knocked on the door and woke me up. He's okay and not hurt, but I don't know how, and he wants to take a walk and talk," I finish talking, dropping unceremoniously onto my bed.

I didn't know Zoey's eyes could get any bigger.

I hop up off my bed rushing to my dresser. "I told him I was going to throw on some clothes and meet him outside. Is this crazy? It feels crazy."

"It's definitely crazy, but you better get your ass out there and find out what's up. You've been kinda crazy about him," she says with that stupid eyebrow wiggle she does.

"Okay, right. It's definitely crazy, but I'm just gonna talk to him and see what's up. What could go wrong?"

When I've finally gotten myself together, in my favorite black flare leggings, a comfy pink hoodie, and a wild silver messy bun, I rush outside.

He's waiting under the tree just outside the dorm building with two drinks in his hands that were not there before, and he seems to have lost Benny. He notices me glancing around for him and points towards the courtyard that connects all the dorms. I see Benny lounging on the edge of the small concrete wall, waving when he sees me, so I give him a small wave in return.

Nodding, I walk towards Roman on shaky legs.

"I wasn't sure what you liked, so I got a caramel macchiato and a hot cocoa," he says, nodding to each Cool Beans cup. He looks unsure of himself, which looks adorable on this gorgeous mammoth of a man.

"I love both, but if I drink that coffee right now, I won't get to sleep again until tomorrow." I say with a small smile as he hands me the hot cocoa.

He takes a sip of the coffee as he slowly starts to walk away. I follow his lead, also sipping on my cocoa. It's the perfect mix of temperature and creamy chocolate goodness. A small moan of contentment slips out, and he freezes.

"As much as I love that sound, if you could refrain until we've discussed everything, that would be very helpful," he says, his voice somehow even more gravelly than before.

I release a nervous giggle, "Soooo, um, can we start with the questions I blurted at you back at the dorm?" Still slightly nervous about walking around with a practical stranger in the middle of the night, I glance around and see a few different groups of other students. One group looks to be studying and the other looks like they might have had a few drinks and thought it was a good time to play football. No one told me that college kids were so nocturnal.

"I'm okay. I'll explain how, later."

"You were definitely not okay. I was there. I saw how hard you were hit. You should not be okay. I mean, I'm glad you are, but how is that possible?"

He smiles before he says, "I know it doesn't make sense right now, but I promise I'm really okay. And I'll tell you everything soon."

"That's not strange or anything . . ." *What am I doing? I am in so over my head right now.* "Okay, so um, what did you want to talk about?"

"Well, you, actually. I'm sure you've noticed I seem to be . . . drawn to you," he says cryptically.

"Umm okay, what a . . . what about me?"

He stops us, takes my cup, turns and sets them both on a bench. He turns back to me again, scratching the back of his neck, "Sorry I'm not good at this, um, can we start with your name? I feel like I'm at a bit of a disadvantage since you know mine." The crooked smile on his face makes my heart feel all fluttery.

"Oh, of course! I never really got to introduce myself to you after the whole . . . uh . . . you know what, never mind." I wave it off with another nervous giggle. *God I sound like an airhead.* Gathering a steadying breath, "Let's start over. Hi, Roman. I'm Leera."

18
ROMAN

*L*eera. My wolf and I seem to sigh in unison. It's perfect. Fuck. She's perfect. She's so tiny, though. The top of her head lands between my chest and shoulders, causing her to have to crane her neck to look me in the eyes. Imogen wasn't this small; she was only five or six inches shorter than me. *Shit, I have to stop comparing them.*

"Good evening, Leera," I say, lifting her petite hand to my lips for another gentle kiss.

The red blush that covers her face looks amazing with her silver hair and icy blue eyes.

"Even though we're starting over, I still want to apologize for your first impression of me. You took my, I mean me, by surprise."

She's still blushing, but she lowers her chin again after nodding. "Leera, you never have to lower your eyes from me," I say gently as I pull her back up until we're making eye contact again. She will be my Luna, my equal, and I will bow before her before I ask her to bow to me.

"Oh . . . okay," she stammers. *Where did my rambling little vixen go?*

"Are you okay? You seemed to have a lot more to say when we weren't intentionally talking," I ask with concern, raising my wolf's hackles.

"Um, I think so . . ." She seems to be thinking of what to say, so I wait patiently. "I don't know how to explain what's going on without sounding crazy," she says, as she starts to lower her eyes but catches herself and looks back up sheepishly.

Goddess, she's adorable. "You can tell me anything, and I will never think you're crazy," I tell her with the upmost sincerity, which seems to make her eyes twinkle.

"Um . . . okay . . . uh," she says as she fidgets with her fingers.

"Leera, if it helps, I know you're probably feeling strange things right now, maybe the last couple weeks. If that's what you're nervous about, we can talk about it," I say as lightly as I can.

She looks shocked for a moment, narrows her eyes a little, and nods. She takes a really deep breath and starts talking so fast that I have to pay close attention to keep up, "Okay, so you're right, I have been feeling really weird lately, mostly ever since I met you, and that first day at the arena, I can't even explain to you how I felt, and then when you touched me, my body got even weirder because it felt like electricity was zapping around my body, and sometimes it feels like I'm not alone in my body, and I don't know what's wrong with me, but something's not right!"

As she finishes getting it all off her mind, her chest is heaving, and her eyes are wide. Taking her in again, and focusing, I agree. I feel something other than the mate bond, and I don't know what's going on. *Benny, there is something more going on with my mate and it doesn't feel human.*

"Great, you definitely think I'm crazy," she mumbles when I realize I haven't responded to her confession.

"No. No, that's not it." I try to reach for her elbow, but she pulls away, and she's starting to hyperventilate. "Hey, hey, shhhhh, it's okay," I say.

She's definitely about to freak out. "Leera, can I hold you to help you calm down?"

Her eyes give away her panic as she allows me to wrap my whole body around her small frame. "Deep breath, my little miracle, whatever it is will be okay," I whisper in her hair as I run my hands up and down her back while she calms.

I can feel Benny approaching. *I can feel it too, Boss. What's going on?*

I wish I knew. The mate bond feels like this shimmering cord connecting us. Right now, it feels like light tugging because we haven't solidified the bond. When complete, it will be a tight, solid connection between us. This other feeling, it feels like . . . it can't be. I continue to hold her. I'm alternating between whispering to Leera and catching Benny up on what she said.

I'm drowning in her spun sugar and honeysuckle scent when she finally starts to calm but the calm only lasts a moment.

19
Leera

In Roman's arms, I have never felt so safe and secure. Which is weird because I always felt safe with my parents. Just his presence surrounding me, his large hands rubbing my back, and the overwhelming smell of cherries and leather—I can't explain the calmness that's settled within me. This should be weird. I just met this man. I've never even had a boyfriend, and here I am in the middle of the night, in a famous hockey player's arms. Yeah, this isn't weird at all, but somehow it feels *right*. Like all my panic attacks and anxiety can't get through this wall of a man.

I'm only allowed a moment of calm, apparently, though.

My body starts to burn. "Roman, something's wrong, more wrong, BIG WRONG!" I try not to scream.

My skin feels like it's on fire. Not the snuggly kind, like you're lying in front of an actual fire. No. I feel like my whole body was thrown into a bonfire and sprinkled with some kind of fuel.

I lose the battle with not screaming and crumble into a

heap on the ground. Roman is instantly kneeling right next to me, pushing my hair out of my face, asking what's wrong as Benny makes his way over to us.

"M-my skin feels like it's on fire. I c-can't catch my breath." I barely get out.

Roman's eyes are wild with panic, and I think that scares me even more.

Just as I'm about to try to reach for him, the fire is replaced by trembling, and it feels like—*that doesn't make any sense—I've finally lost my mind.*

I swear, my body just growled. Not my stomach. My body. *What the hell?*

"Help me. There's something inside of me. My body it . . ." I trail off, unable to finish the sentence. I'll be committed. This isn't happening. I knew his showing up was too good to be true. I was dreaming, and now I'm having a nightmare. Whatever *this* is, it can't be real.

Both of Roman's knees crash to the ground, getting as close to me as he can without touching me completely, like he's worried he'll hurt me. He tenderly wraps my trembling hands in his. "Leera, no matter how crazy it sounds, talk to me. What's going on?"

The concern in his eyes seems to rip away any sense of self-preservation I had left.

"I swear something in my body just . . . growled. I know it's crazy. I don't know what's happening. What's wrong with me? I'm pretty sure I'm having a nightmare, but this feels so real."

The men share a worried and confused look, but it almost looks like Roman is trying not to smile, like he's had some kind of "ah-ha" moment.

"Why would you smile like that? Oh my god, did you do this?! Did you drug me?!"

"No. Of course not. I would never do anything to harm you in any way. Ever," he says frantically. "Hey, look at me. I promise we'll find out what's going on, and you'll be okay."

I try to nod, but the fire returns with vengeance. Before I can stop it, a wail escapes me, and Roman has me scooped up into his arms, and he's jogging away from the school.

He wouldn't drug me, right? But is he kidnapping me now? "Please make it stop." I cry through the pain.

He nuzzles the top of my head with his nose, yes, nuzzles, as he whispers kind words that everything will be okay. I look over to Benny and he looks torn between worry and excitement. These men are so weird. I feel like my body is on fire, I might have been drugged, but for some totally crazy reason, I trust them to take care of me.

"We're going to take you home with us and have our hea— doctor come check on you, Leera. Is that okay? You don't have to do anything you don't want to do, but I want to take care of you."

All I can do is nod when he looks at me like that as we approach a giant black SUV. Benny runs ahead of us and opens the door. I expect Roman to set me down in the seat, but instead, he ducks my head and scoots into the seat, still cradling my little body in his so that I'm sitting in his lap and resting my head on his chest.

I wish I wasn't in so much pain so I could enjoy this moment.

Benny slams the door, runs all the way around, and jumps into the driver's seat. He throws the car in gear, and before I have time to think, we're flying down the road.

My body continues to alternate between feeling like I was thrown into a burning building, being electrocuted, and dropped in the arctic tundra. Whatever's happening can't be good. I sound like an idiot whimpering and wailing in this god of a man's arms, but my body is out of my control at this point.

We pull up to what has to be the largest townhouse in the area, built on top of a personal parking garage. Roman doesn't wait for Benny to open the door for us. Instead, he flies out of the SUV before it's even been put in park. He enters a number on the pin pad of the elevator, and we're quickly ascending.

We're met by the rest of the starting Predators' line-up. I wasn't exactly expecting an audience for the weirdest, most painful moment of my life.

"Doc is ten minutes away," one of the twins says with an ornery look on his face.

The scary-looking one that's the goalie shoves him out of the way and says, "I got a room ready for her."

Roman rushes down the hallway, never taking his eyes off mine.

He enters one of the rooms and tries to gently lay me on the bed, but I find myself latching onto him. "Please don't leave me," I whimper, knotting my hands in his shirt.

"I wasn't going to leave you, Little Miracle; I was going to sit right next to you, but if this is what you want, then this is what you get," he says with a small smile.

He's called me that twice now. Why am I a miracle?

I'm not able to think any more about it when a sweet little old lady comes in. "Hi dearie, I'm Matilda, you can call me Tilly if you like. The healer is coming in now, but you just holler if you need anything," she says as she scurries away.

"Healer?" I question. I would say more if I could, but my body isn't exactly listening to my instructions at the moment. Roman just grunts in response as another older woman comes in; this one isn't as cute as Miss Tilly, though.

"Well, hello there . . ." the woman says with a raised eyebrow as she looks at Roman. "Jeanine, this is Leera," he says as they just stare at each other for a moment.

"Well, let's see what we can do about the strange feelings you're having," the woman, Jeanine, says. "Roman, can you set her down so I can take a look at her?"

"Only if she wants to," he turns his eyes on me, "is that okay? I promise, I'll be right here. She's here to help."

I whimper and nod. He so carefully lowers me onto the softest bed I've ever laid on. Another thing I wish I could enjoy right now. The doctor begins feeling my body in different places before breaking out her stethoscope.

Her evaluation seems to take forever, but no one speaks. The only sounds in the rooms are my grunts and whimpers, and I think Roman might have growled. I don't even know anymore. My body has also calmed a bit since I laid down. I still don't feel great, but I don't feel like I'm burning alive.

"Well, honey, it looks like you're going to be just fine," she says, like everything is right as rain.

"Excuse me? H-how is this fine? What was that?" I screech, not even being able to enjoy that I'm feeling a little better every minute because this lady is obviously crazy.

Roman and Jeanine seem to share a silent conversation as she turns and leaves the room.

"Where is she going?!" I begin to panic again before he

closes the door. "Wh-what are you doing?"

"Leera, we need to talk, and it's going to sound crazy, but I beg you to just hear me out," he says hesitantly, retaking his seat next to the bed and gathering my hands in his again as he continues to talk, "Has anything happened to you recently? Something out of the ordinary? Where did you grow up? How much family do you have?"

Not sure what else to do, I give him my entire life story, up until he knocked on my door.

He just stares at me for a minute and says, "Uh. Okay. We'll figure the rest out later, but there's no easy way for me to tell you this, and you're probably not going to believe me," he says calmly.

"Umm, okay, whatever it is, please just tell me."

"It looks like you might not be human," he says low and even.

I laugh so hard that I choke on my spit, which causes my whole body to hurt again. When I've finally finished coughing, he's just looking at me. "Wait, you think you're serious?" I ask with a nervous laugh.

His only response is a clipped nod.

"You say that like not being a human is even an option?!" I ask as the door opens and his teammates re-enter the room.

The last man to walk in the room is named Andrei, I think. Our eyes meet, his eyes go wide, and there's some kind of weird energy between us. It's not like the feelings I get with Roman, but there's some there.

Is this really happening? Could I be more than just an awkward orphan girl?

I'm lost in my thoughts when I hear Benny's voice say, "Hey

Leera, I know this is a lot, but we're all here for you. We'll always be here for you from now on. Roman has some crazy stuff to tell you, and we hope you'll keep an open mind and trust us." He's so calm and kind that I just nod.

"I feel a little weird, but for some reason I do trust you. All of you. This is so weird. I know I shouldn't; I really do," I say as I make eye contact with each of them. "All logic and stranger danger are pretty well out the window at this point . . . so okay . . . I'm listening," I finish quietly.

The smile that lights up Roman's face is worth it; no matter how weird this is, it makes me smile a little too.

"Okay, how would you like us to discuss this? With all of us, or just me?" Roman asks.

"I think I'm okay with all of you unless anyone has other things to do; I don't want to keep anyone from their own stuff just because of me."

"Nah, we're good right here," the twins say at the same time. They look much too excited about all of this.

"Okayyy . . . can you please just tell me what's going on?" I ask looking around the room before my eyes lock onto Roman's.

The air gets a little thick with tension as I can see him physically working himself up to whatever it is he needs to tell me.

"Okay, I think it's easiest to start with giving you the knowledge that almost all creatures you've read about in books, or seen in movies, are real."

I wait for the punch line, but it never comes. They're all still super serious. Not one smile was cracked. Maybe this really is just some crazy realistic dream, but I promised to listen, so whatever.

"Ha, I'll just have to take your word for that one."

Roman just nods before he continues, "For example, pretty much all professional athletes in the world aren't entirely human."

My eyes widen in realization of what he's just said and when I look around the room this time, it's a little more hesitant, and I lose my grasp on the nervous laugh I was trying to hold in. The twins are smiling even wider than usual, so instead of speaking I just nod.

"Hockey is primarily played by werewolves and other men with werewolf blood."

My eyes somehow widen even further. I'm either sitting in a room full of crazy people, or a room full of werewolves. *You've definitely lost your mind, Leera.*

A small laugh escapes me, and I offer another small nod for him to continue, I mean what the hell am I supposed to say to that?

"A lot of the folklore is based on the truth. How much do you know about werewolves?"

"Um, I mean, silver bullets; you shift under a full moon; alphas are the boss. Oh! I love Twilight. I was always Team Jacob." I nearly facepalm myself the second I say that. That sounded way less stupid in my head.

They all sigh, grumble, and scoff at once. Roman is rubbing his forehead, the twins are snickering, and Slate looks disgusted, causing a nervous giggle to escape me.

"The silver is true. It's one of the very few things that can kill us. The full moon is only partially true, our first transformation is under a full moon. The werewolf hierarchy is true, I am the Alpha of our pack, but like that horrid movie," he continues as though it pains him to agree with it, so I press my lips together to keep from smiling.

He chuckles at whatever my expression reveals, and I can feel the sound throughout my entire body. *That was weird, but also felt amazing. . .*

"Anyways, we can change into our wolf form any time we want. We don't *imprint*," he says the word with contempt, and I lose the war with holding in a less nervous giggle. "We have something far more important. Most supernatural creatures do. For us, the Moon Goddess bestows every wolf a fated mate. It's the other half of our soul. The person you can't live without. Most wolves are mated to other wolves, but a mate can be any other living soul," he says this with a sadness, longing and vulnerability I don't understand.

"I was given my mate a long time ago," he begins, and just when I think he won't say more, he continues, "She was . . . taken from me, but that's a story for another day. I was always taught that you are only given one mate." He slowly lifts his head to stare straight at me, "Until I met you."

Again, all the air is pulled from the room and my hand instinctively rests on my heart as I stare at this man, trying to absorb what he's telling me.

"Leera, that day at the arena, when we were supposed to do the first interview . . . the reason I reacted that way, was from shock. I thought someone had spelled or cursed me. That feeling you felt, or at least some of why you feel this way, is our mate bond. Our souls are woven together. We were made to live our lives together," he must misunderstand my small gasp as fear when he lifts his hands in surrender and quickly adds, "that doesn't mean you have to have anything to do with me. You can reject the bond, though painful, and you don't ever have to see me again," he quickly adds. Even the thought of rejecting him feels like a fracture to the very core of my being, though I still cannot speak, I'm waiting for him to finish.

"I had never heard of anyone getting a second chance with their mate, but after speaking with our elders, it is possible, just very rare. I was in shock, and I can admit I was terrified, especially with you being a human. But after tonight, I don't know how it's possible, but the healer was able to sense a wolf within you. I don't know how you've lived your whole life without knowing about her."

"Her?" I ask before the thought was even able to cross my mind.

"Mmhmm," he nods, "Your wolf. Your wolf will be a female, like ours are males."

"Oh, right, that makes sense," I reply a little embarrassed at my lack of common sense.

"None of that. You never have to be embarrassed around any of us. We'll answer all your questions and support you in any way you need."

All the men nod, seemingly happy I haven't bolted from the room yet. Andrei comes back and seems to have pulled himself together but the strange look he gives me tells me something is still bothering him. Miss Tilly is right on his heels with a tray of snacks and teacups.

"I wasn't sure what you liked, so I brought a little bit of everything. You'll need to keep your energy up," she says sweetly as she slaps Benny's hand away from my smorgasbord of snacks making me smile.

"Thank you, so much. This looks amazing," I say, taking in all the treats when Roman reclaims my attention.

"What questions do you have? For me. For us. Ask anything you want."

Swallowing my snack and washing it down with a yummy citrusy tea, I nod.

"Um, okay so . . . I'm your soulmate, er mate?"

Nod.

"Our souls were made for each other?"

Nod.

"I'm not a human?"

Shake.

"I have a . . . I'm a werewolf?"

Nod.

"How?"

"We'll have to figure that out together, but rest assured we will."

"So that growling feeling? Why did I feel like I was dying?" I ask cautiously.

"Your wolf seems to have been locked inside of you for a very long time. She wants to come out. Our first shift is unfortunately unpleasant, and usually on a full moon as I mentioned before. Some have their first shift as early as four years old, and the latest I've seen was thirteen. The later that first shift is, the more uncomfortable it is. Because she's been trapped for so long, she tried to force the shift unnaturally. She's also probably overwhelmed between wanting to be released and my presence," he explains.

I just continue to nod and nibble on my snacks, sharing them with Benny and the twins. If everything wasn't weird enough, can you picture the most gorgeous men you've ever seen, who are also werewolves, sipping out of teacups and having snacks? I'm literally having a tea party with a bunch of hockey playing werewolves, until a thought crosses my mind, "So um, I don't want to mess with my wolf right now, that hurt really bad but um . . ." I trail off.

"He meant it darlin', ask us anything," Benny presses.

Looking only at Roman, I gather my courage to ask, "Can I-can I see your wolf? For two reasons really. One, I need some confirmation that this is happening, even if it's a dream. Two, if this is really happening, I really want to see him."

The way Roman's face lights up, tells me everything I need to know before he springs from his chair, "Okay, but let's go up to the roof, do you feel up to it? This is a small room and might be a little cramped for my wolf."

Full of excitement, even if this is crazy, I hop out of bed a little too quickly on my wobbly legs. Roman notices and scoops me up into a cradle again. Lightning shoots through my skin everywhere we touch, which is currently pretty much everywhere. If it's really always like this, I may never want to walk on my own again.

"I got you little one," he says as he nuzzles the top of my head before dropping a tiny kiss to my forehead. I melt even further into his arms when I realize that the nuzzling makes a lot more sense now. *This is crazy. But . . .I kind of love it. I hope I'm not dreaming after all.*

Roman and I finally burst through the door to their rooftop oasis, and he gently sets me down. I was expecting your everyday drab and dark rooftop, but I guess I should remember to expect more from these men. There's a large fire pit surrounded by comfy-looking outdoor couches in the far corner. There's a small greenhouse to my left that looks to be full of all kinds of plant life. And in the corner opposite the fire pit is a giant hot tub.

While I've been taking in my surroundings, Roman has moved to the center of the roof and peeled off his shirt.

My eyes take in all of the man before me and for whatever reason, it all makes perfect sense. I knew a man like this couldn't possibly be human. He looks like a god standing before me with the stars twinkling above us. He smirks like he can read my thoughts, and I'm just thankful not to be drooling. He lets me finish looking over the ridges of all his muscles before he breaks the spell I was under.

"Are you sure you're ready for this?" he asks with that perfectly gravelly voice.

Another small nod, returned by one of his own.

In barely a moment, his body stretches, elongates, snaps, crunches, sprouts fur, and grows to an unexpected size. *The size is another thing Twilight got surprisingly correct; I wonder if a real werewolf was part of the movie production. Or maybe they used real werewolves even, and made up the CGI stuff?*

The large cream-colored wolf before me is the most beautiful creature I've ever seen, and I've seen a lot. I've been all over the world looking at the most amazing creatures on the entire planet, and none of them even come close. His mismatched, green and blue eyes stand out even more brightly against his fluffy cream fur.

He approaches me slowly, with his head lowered a bit, since my body doesn't seem to want to move. I keep telling myself this isn't happening. There's just no way this is happening, right?! But I can see it with my own eyes. I can feel it in my soul.

As soon as he's within reach, I regain control of my body, and lift my hand to his snout that sits right at eye level with me.

His whole body melts under my touch. The tingling feeling of us touching still happening while he's a freaking wolf. His fur is nothing like I expected. I expected thick, coarse hair, more similar to a wild wolf. I have never been happier to be wrong. It's soft and fluffy and warm as I run my hand up and along the top of his head and in between his ears. Bringing my other arm around, I hug him, and it feels like everything in the world is just *right.*

Mate, a voice in my mind says, startling me backwards, causing a small whine to escape the magnificent creature in front of me. He nudges my hand with his nose, seeming to ask for an explanation.

"Uh, there was a voice in my mind . . . it . . .er she . . . said mate."

While I feel like a crazy person, Roman is excited enough his tail is wagging, and his front paws are doing that tappy-dance that dogs do when they're happy. This causes a chain reaction of giggles from me, nuzzles from him, and then more giggles.

We're interrupted by the door swinging open and an irritated Benny coming through and staring directly at Roman, having another silent conversation. *Don't legends say they can speak to each other telepathically? I'll have to ask about that.*

Benny comes forward with a pair of pants and Roman snatches them from him before I've fully processed that he's human again. *Holy shit. I think I just saw his dick.* I can feel my cheeks turning red, so I turn around as quickly as I can while he dresses. Liquid fire is spreading throughout my body. *Is this a werewolf thing or a really turned-on thing?*

"Leera, do you trust me?" he asks, his voice suddenly very serious and . . . worried? Just like that, it feels like someone dumped a bucket of ice water over my head.

I nod, but my worry must be all over my face when he sighs.

"Someone is here and I'm begging you to ignore her, and anything that comes out of her mouth."

My eyes narrow and I can only nod again but the worry has settled in the bottom of my stomach. It doesn't help that Benny won't even look at me.

My heart is soaring. For the first time in so fucking long, I am *happy.*

Until Benny crashes through the rooftop door with that look on his face. I had the walls up on my mind, while I had this moment with my miracle mate, and apparently that was the wrong decision.

The moment I let my walls come down I'm assaulted with a barrage of voices, all my men, furious.

What's going on?!

Everyone but Benny quiets.

India is here, he says as he walks across the roof with a pair of joggers for me. Wolves are used to nudity. We don't keep our clothes during a shift so while it's normal for us, I'm thankful Benny is already so thoughtful of Leera. I don't want to overwhelm or embarrass her. Not yet anyways.

What does she want? I ask, irritated that my moment with Leera is being interrupted. Fuck, how am I going to deal with this?

You, Boss, what else does she ever want? Slate replies obnoxiously.

Fuck off, keep her busy until I can get Leera settled and away from her.

That's not going to work, Boss. She's standing in between the kitchen and living room; there's no getting around her. She won't budge. She's all worked up and won't leave until she sees you.

FUCK! Okay. All hands-on deck, I'm going to bring her in with me. We're not telling India who she is, and I am going to try not to show my feelings.

Grunting is their only response until Benny pipes up, *You sure that's a good idea?*

Probably not but it's all I have right now.

"Leera, do you trust me?" I ask in a far more serious tone than I intended. *Dammit.*

She gives me a small nod, but her body language changes immediately, and I can feel her anxious energy rising already. This is going to be absolute torture.

"Someone is here and I'm begging you to ignore her and anything that comes out of her mouth."

Her eyes narrow and she barely nods. I know I just lost so much progress with her and it's making my heart ache.

Benny, I want her to go down with you. She's your priority until I get India out of here.

Another clipped nod and I can tell he's also going to be pissed at me for this.

"Leera, you're going to go in and stay with Benny please," I say as softly as I can.

Her eyebrows push together, and still only offers a small nod. My heart is shredding at having to push her away when I've only just got to touch her.

I walk through the door and down the stairs ahead of them, back into the townhouse. I'm immediately unsettled when we get inside and my home that was just full of my mate's scent is now clouded by India's.

She's standing there with her hands on her hips, glaring at the twins. When we all come into view, she quickly sheds her bitchy exterior and shifts gears into a sweet and innocent act. Little does she know, what little patience I had for her before has been completely eviscerated by having a second chance with my mate.

"What do you want?" I ask before she has a chance to say a word.

"I just . . ." she trails off as Benny comes in with Leera wearing his hoodie, and while my wolf lividly snarls under my skin, I know what he's doing, as much as I hate it. He's covering my scent. The thought infuriates me, even though I know it's needed to get through this without incident.

"Well, well, Benjamin, I didn't peg you for picking up a runt," she laughs while every man in the room snarls out loud at her, startling both her and Leera.

Fuck. Benny is whispering in her ear that it's okay and to remember what I said. Pride wells in my chest that my men are already so protective of her.

India struts across the room in her tight red dress, reaching out for me as she nears. "I've missed y . . ." She stops as I swat her hand away from me. Her eyes seem to catch fire for a moment before she remembers herself. "India, you need to leave. I'll talk to you later."

"But I just got here, and I haven't seen you in so long. I saw the hit at the game and came straight here to take care of you." She pouts, causing a sharp gasp from Leera.

Benny tries to lead her away, but she refuses. *Great, she's a stubborn little thing.* Then her icy blue eyes seem to shoot frozen daggers at me, while mine implore her to trust me, but it only melts her a fraction.

"I'm fine, India. You need to leave," I say again.

"But I didn't do anything wrong," she screeches and stomps her foot, arms now crossed over her chest. "I came to be here for you, and this is how you treat me just because Benny found himself a little whore to bring home?!"

My feet are moving before my brain can react. In a fraction of a second, I'm in her face, nearly nose to nose as I snarl, "You will never speak about her like that again. Do you understand me?" She frantically nods and whimpers, but I can't find a fuck to give. "NOW. GET. OUT. Of my house!"

She finally takes the hint and runs from the room, still fuming.

As soon as the door slams shut, I run to Leera and drop to my knees where she stands beside Benny crying quietly. The men all gasp clearly in shock. I go to my knees for no one. Well, one other. Until now. Until her. "Leera, please, please look at me."

"Can you please just take me home?" she whimpers, still refusing to make eye contact. Her hands are knotted together, and the tears falling from her eyes have my soul splintering to the floor.

With a lump in my throat, I rise to my feet, "Yes, of course. I'm so sorry you had to go through that. Andrei can you get the car?" He nods.

"Can I ride with you?" I ask softly. She only lightly nods, so

I go to my room to finish dressing myself.

Leera is saying goodbye to Matilda when I return with a shirt on, and she still won't look at me.

"Please let me explain?" I practically beg.

"Roman, I think you've explained plenty tonight, okay? It's after one o'clock in the morning. In case you forgot, it's been a really long day and I have a lot of information to process. Please, just take me home."

And with her words, my wolf begins to howl, and I want to join him.

We all ride in silence, and I pray to the Goddess that this isn't it, that she doesn't hate me, and we can get past this. Please don't let her reject me. Give me a chance to make this right.

21
India

Releasing an angry screech, I stomp up to the car as my driver opens the door.

"What can I do for you Madam India?" the ancient man asks.

"You can shut the door, shut up, drive, and leave me alone," I snap.

What the hell just happened? I know I'm not Roman's favorite person, but I thought we'd been finding a rhythm. After Daddy told his father about the king's plans, I thought things would get better.

I thought he'd be excited about being a King.

Not just some commander and hockey player.

He was always meant for so much more.

And I *will* be his queen.

I can't help the sinister smile that overtakes my face.

I'm going to be a queen. A QUEEN. A fucking queen.

And then, the rest of our plans can finally take shape.

If I could just find a way to help him get over his little

commoner mate, everything would be so much simpler. I mean it was over five hundred years ago that our fathers got rid of the bitch. You'd think he'd move on already.

ERH! I'm so glad I haven't found my mate. I don't want or need one. If I found him, I'd just have to reject him. I'm not giving up being the QUEEN for something as basic as a soulmate.

Sighing, I flop back onto the leather seats of the town car Daddy bought for that decrepit old man to drive me around in. He tells me his name all the time, but I always forget to remember. Not that it really matters.

Ugh and what about that little bitch of Benny's. Her fake silver hair and innocent act with the tears, what was that about? Oh, wouldn't it be rich if that pitiful little human was his mate? The thought causes me to truly laugh for a moment.

With one more sigh, I start thinking of ways I can make Roman happy about our marriage.

Maybe someday I could even make him love me, but if not, that's okay.

Who needs love when you get to marry a King.

22
Leera

I know he tried to warn me ahead of time, that someone was going to upset me, and I thought I was prepared, but nothing in the world could have prepared me for *India*.

Just the thought of her name sets my blood to boiling. She was tall, and sophisticated, and classy, but ugh, WHAT A BITCH?!

The way she just talks about people like they're not even there.

And she seemed to want Roman. Do they have something going on? Of course they do! Look at him! Of course he'd have someone like that by his side. Someone of his caliber. He must have left me with Benny so I wouldn't embarrass him.

I'm drowning in negative thoughts in the back seat of the giant SUV. I can feel his eyes on me but why even bother? He has his hands full with that putrid woman. Why would he bother with me?

What if none of this is even real? What if in my weird pain induced situation, I hallucinated the whole thing? I mean, come on! Werewolves, soulmates, me not being human. Ha!

That's got to be it. I imagined the whole thing.

Then why can I still feel the tiny fissure in my heart when she reached for him just minutes after our moment on the roof.

It all felt so real. I can still feel his fur between my fingers. I can still feel the electricity that bounded through my body when he touched me. Held me. The healer. Miss Tilly. The guys.

I notice too late that I'm spiraling. It feels like there's a boulder on my chest, and I can't get a full breath.

"Leera, can I please come to the backseat with you to calm you down," Roman asks from his seat with worry all over his stupid gorgeous face.

I can't get enough air to speak, so I just shake my head remembering to keep my scowl in place. I'm mad at him. But none of that helps the panic settling deep into my body. The pressure on my chest continues to grow, I'm getting lightheaded, and the trembling is starting. Why do I have to be such a freak of nature? And I'm not even talking about being a freaking were-wolf! I'm talking about this horrible affliction in my body. Why can't I control my own mind and body? Why does it take off on its own and render me unable to function? To think I took for granted my freedom before the crippling anxiety set in. How do I get back to that place?

I'm lost to the throes of anxiety when I hear his voice cut through the haze, "Baby please, I'm coming back there, I'm sorry if that upsets you, but I can't just sit here and watch you strug-gling like this," he says as he starts wedging and shoving his mas-sive body between the two front seats, to get to me. It would be funny if I wasn't angry with him and in mid panic attack.

I try to scoot to the window to get away but by the time

he's fully seated himself beside me, he takes up most of the entire back seat, leaving only enough space for me.

"Shhhh, it's okay," he coos as he scoops me back into his arms and damn my body for melting into him. I don't want comfort and electric pulses when I'm angry. "I'm so sorry she upset you and you had to see that, if you would just let me explain."

At the mention of *her* I finally find my voice and let it all out, "No Roman, I don't want you to explain. Don't you think it would have been important, before you started preaching soulmates, that you tell me you are already with someone?! Someone like that?! Someone who could not be further away from everything I am and will ever be?!"

I'm getting a little hysterical, but I don't care right now. "You spend the evening turning my entire world upside down, but you don't have a moment to tell me about her?! WAIT?! You said you already knew I was your soulmate, and you didn't break up with her?! What, were you waiting to see what I would say so you could keep her if I turned you down?!" We're pulling up in front of my dorm building now.

"You know what, Roman, just don't." He tries to hold me tighter and opens his mouth to speak before snapping it back shut. "I don't know how things work in the werewolf world, but I grew up in the human world," I'm shouting now as I throw the door open and begin climbing from the vehicle. "I don't want to talk to you right now. And if you think you can just tell me I'm your soulmate and that magically means I'm all yours with no work, you are dead wrong," I say, stepping back up to the car to jab my finger in his rock-hard chest. *Focus, Leera.*

"My parents might be gone now, but they taught me my worth. If you want me, you have to work for me and prove yourself. I will not be falling into your arms and immediately living happily ever after, like some kind of fairytale." With that, I slam the door and sprint to my dorm building without another look back.

The amount of life altering crazy shit that can happen in a matter of hours is just ridiculous.

As I sneak back into my dorm room and find Zoey and everything just as I left it. I feel like I was sucked into some kind of twilight zone. I mean I left here mere hours ago, in awe of a giant hockey god, just little ol' boring me. The weirdest thing about me was the color of my hair for fuck's sake.

I plug my phone in, turn it off, and change back into my silk jammies, realizing I'm not the same girl that climbed out of them.

I'd like to play stupid and pretend none of that ever happened but there's no use lying to myself. I can feel it all in the fiber of my being.

I am a werewolf. This is the first moment I've had to myself to really think about it all. The weird feelings. The magnetic pull to Roman. That strange growling I feel. There is another being within me. A strong and powerful wolf. *I bet she's beautiful.*

Can you hear me? I don't know how any of this works, but I thought I'd say hi, now that I know you exist. I don't even know if you can speak but I feel bad that you've been so neglected. You've been here my whole life, and I never knew. Um, I also want to apologize ahead of time, I have a bit of a tendency to ramble. Wait, do you know that? Have you been like buried deep within me? Or just under the skin trapped? Gosh this is a lot.

I wait for her to respond. For a minute I think I feel something, but nothing comes. I sigh and climb back into bed; I try to settle but my life has completely changed. I won't be able to avoid Roman and the guys for long. I have to learn how to *be* a werewolf. Are there rules? I'm so far out of my element.

Wait?! Sitting up so fast my head spins, "Were my parents werewolves?" I whisper out loud. *Did they know I was a werewolf?*

With too many thoughts and emotions swirling through my mind, I force myself to lie back down in bed, even if I'm not able to sleep, I know I need to rest. There's nothing I can do about anything right now but allow the tears to flow.

The dark sky begins to lighten when I'm finally pulled into a fitful sleep.

23
ROMAN

The moment she slams the door in my face every terror and fear comes slamming into me with the force of a freight train.

Losing Imogen, the moment I saw Leera, thinking she was human and would reject me, and now, after everything I've been through, she still might reject me, over INDIA?!

Releasing the deafening roar from my soul should make me feel better, but it does little to numb the venomous fear coursing through my veins.

Benny is trying to console me, but I can't hear anything over the thundering of my heart. My wolf is howling and trying to rip me apart from the inside out.

How can I give her space when I can't breathe without her? I thought I had been breathing just fine the last five hundred years, but I didn't know how wrong I was until she let me hold her.

With the rest of my soul re-intact, I took the first full breath in half a fucking millennium. I can't just let her walk away. I can't let this be all we are. I don't want to live a half-life without her. I can't.

I replay her parting words over and over in my mind. I have to work for her. What kind of work does she want? How much is enough? How much is too much? It doesn't matter, I'll do anything and everything to make her happy. Hopefully, sooner rather than later but all I have is time.

I immediately start planning all the things I can do to show her that while the base of our bond is a fated soul bond, I care about her and will learn everything about her and worship her in every way.

I've never really had to court a woman. I think it's called dating now. As a werewolf, you usually find your mate and that's it. Sure, we spend time together, get to know one another and such, but it's instant. Then having spent the centuries arranged to be married, I don't even know where to start. I do the only thing I can think of, and I search "things that make women happy" in the search engine on my phone.

I don't have her phone number, which is frustrating because I want to text her, just to apologize and say good night. Do I have Slate get her number for me so I can talk to her, or is that crossing a line?

Why does this have to be so complicated?!

"Benny, how do you handle all the human women?" I ask from the back seat, feeling defeated.

He's chuckling before I finish my sentence, "Sorry to break it to you, Boss, but I don't have to work for the women I see. They don't really want anything but to be seen on my arm, so I can't help you there."

He turns serious for a moment while he thinks, "If I found

myself in a position to want to really win a woman's heart, though, I would probably start with having Slate run a full background check on them and learn absolutely everything I could about them and build from there."

Well, at least we're on the same page there. I don't think it's acceptable at the human level, but I also don't really give a fuck.

I shoot him a small nod, and he just shakes his head with that stupid shit-eating grin on his face.

As soon as I crash through the front door, it feels so empty. Now that she's been here, her absence is a living, breathing thing. When she was here, it felt like a real *home*. Without her, it's just another building.

My men are gathered at the kitchen island, waiting for me. "What are you going to do? What do you need from us?" Andrei is the first to ask with a spark of determination in his eyes.

"Slate, I need her phone number and any and all information you can get about her." He raises an eyebrow at my instruction, "I don't care how it looks. I need to know everything about her that I can, she'll tell me the rest as we get to know each other," I instruct, allowing myself a small smile at the thought of learning all about my little mate.

"Eris, Dolos, I want you two to take turns keeping an eye on her when I can't while we're here this week. We have two away games, so also make sure you have someone covering her while we're gone. Get with Benny, he already has something in place. I want to make sure she's safe and that she doesn't struggle with her wolf. If ANYTHING happens, I'm to be alerted IMMEDIATELY." They both nod and walk away.

They may seem like great big goof balls, but they are the top spies of the King's werewolf army in Zabella, and their particular set of skills are invaluable.

"Benny, what I need from you is no simple task. Please don't fight me on this. I need you to run interference with India. I don't want to see her, and I don't want her here at all. The away games will help, but with her father's expectations, I need to figure out how to handle this." He's not happy about it, but he also nods and walks away.

"Andrei, you're with me. As we receive intel from Slate, I need your help making sure I don't blunder this whole romantic human stuff." I hate feeling vulnerable about this kind of thing but I'm man enough to admit when I need help. I'll do anything for her.

Andrei looks like he has something to say but leaves when Slate comes back into the room. "Got her number. Figured I'd start with that so you could contact her. I'll get to work on the rest now."

Snatching the number out of his hand, I pull my phone out of my pocket and add her number to my contacts under My Little Mate. I think for a moment . . . if she sees that, she could think that's all she is to me. So, I change it to Leera for now. We have an eternity for fun little pet names.

> Good night, Sunshine.

I text her before going to our gym to burn off the rest of this tension. It looks like it will be another night of no sleep. Being away from her all week, between her demands and away games, it's going to be torture, but I have to at least try to respect her wishes at some kind of level.

24
Leera

I wake with a start as Zoey crashes around the room, complaining that her alarm didn't go off.

What a weird dream. I think to myself, but the chuckle escapes me, causing Zoey to stop her mid-morning tantrum and just stare at me.

"Sorry. I had the weirdest dream," I say, reaching for my phone on my bedside table and powering it back on. "You'll nev . . ." I trail off as I see a text pop up on my phone from an unknown number.

It couldn't have been real! Werewolves?! That bitch. I'm grumbling at my phone about stupid bitches and werewolves when

Zoey coughs, reminding me I was talking to her before I got distracted. "Um, you wouldn't believe me if I told you," I try to placate her but quicker than I realize, she snatches the phone out of my hand.

"OH MY GAWD, YOU LITTLE TRAMP!" She laughs out loud, "You were with ROMAN last night?! We fell asleep watching a movie. How did I miss this?!"

She's practically yelling, and I can't exactly tell if she's excited or angry—maybe a little bit of both.

"Girl, I woke you up! We did fall asleep, and I woke up to knocking on the door, and then he was there, and he wanted to talk, and then . . . and then I think his girlfriend showed up," I say, dropping my head into my hands so she can't see how much it affects me.

"Ohhh, I think I kind of remember you waking me up, but you know how hard I sleep." She laughs it off like it's no big deal, while I'm over here having a small life crisis internally that I can't even tell anyone about because I'm a freaking werewolf!

I can still feel the strange stirring beneath my skin when I do so much as think of him. I'll have to try not to do that so much. *Yeah, like that's gonna happen.*

I'm so glad I chose not to take any Saturday classes, as I watch Zoey fumble around to make it to class on time while I enjoy my pajamas and comfy bed.

When she finally wiggles through the door with her bag and books, she shuts it behind her. The quiet only lasts a second before she opens the door back up enough to pop her head through when she says, "Hey, I don't mean to run off on you. No matter what, everything will be okay. If you still need to get it all out when I'm done with classes, I'm totally game."

I smile and nod as she leaves again and I allow myself to return my attention to my phone which now has another new message.

Unknown

Good Morning Beautiful <3

I can't help the smile that stretches across my face at such simple words. I've never had any real friends, male friends, or even close to a boyfriend. It was always just me and my parents. I'm going to have to find a way to tell him that. He's probably used to fully experienced women and I couldn't be farther from it.

Shaking the thoughts from my head, I add Roman's number to my phone and think for a moment, deciding if I should just use his name or a fun nickname. I tap my finger to my chin in thought for a few moments. Ah ha! I finally have it!

Giggling to myself, and satisfied with his contact name, now I need to decide if I'm going to text him back. I told him to work for it and he's trying. It would be wrong of me to just leave him on read, right? Especially after I kind of blew up on him yesterday. I didn't mean to.

Good Morning.

Short and concise. I'm still upset with him after all. I'm not going to forget all the shit last night over a couple sweet text messages. I've barely hit send, when the little texting bubbles pop up to let me know he's typing.

My Pucking Mate

What's your favorite coffee?

> That's a loaded question, I love all coffee and have been trying lots of new flavors, right now I'm loving The Brunette at the shop by me. It tastes like a Snickers candy bar.

> Got it, you like your coffee as sweet as you are.

> Cheese Level 10/10

I can't help giggling at our conversation as I make my way to the bathroom for my morning routine. I'm so incredibly thankful these dorm rooms have their own bathrooms. I can't imagine having to go to the end of the hall or having to use a public bathroom all the time in general. They remodeled the campus a couple of years ago, so now the dorm rooms are set up more like hotel rooms. Each dorm has a bathroom to share with your roommate. We also each have our desk and shelf built in.

As I walk back into the main room in a towel, there's a knock at the door. "Who is it?" I shout, but there's no response. I slowly check the peep hole, but there's no one there. Curiosity wins and I crack the door open. To my surprise there is a Brunette iced coffee, a hot cocoa, and a single red rose with a note that says,

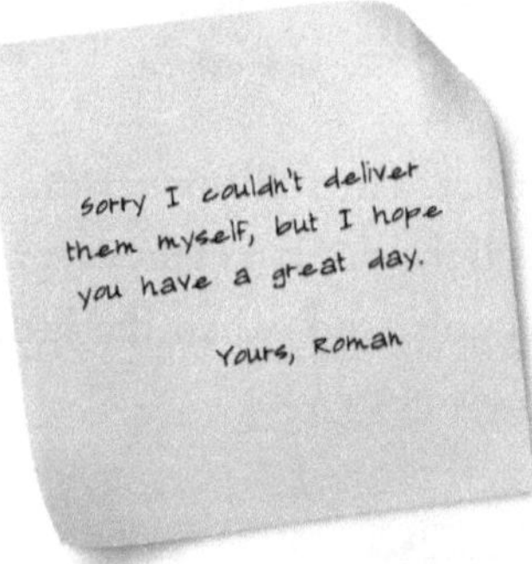

How sweet is that?! Sipping the coffee and smelling the

rose, I walk back over to my bed to grab my phone. I set them on the table and snap a pic to text Roman.

> Omagosh thank you so much! That was so sweet of you! You really didn't have to do that.

My Pucking Mate

> Please let me spoil you. It makes me happy to make you happy.

Gosh how can I say no to that?! Zoey won't believe this. So naturally, I have to text her too. She is my only friend after all.

> Look what I just got.

Zozo

> SQUEEE OMG I'm so jelly

Is this real life? I think to myself while I search the dorm for something to use as a vase, hoping to keep my sweet little rose alive for as long as possible. A red solo cup will have to do for now.

> Really. Thank you. My parents are the only people who have ever bought me anything.

Plopping into my desk chair and setting my phone, drinks, and rose on the desk, I wake my laptop to check the guys' hockey schedule for this week.

To my dismay, it looks like he has two away games before another home game, this time on Saturday. That means he'll probably be gone all week.

I don't have a right to be disappointed since I'm the one who pushed him away. It killed me to do it but come on! The guy tells me I'm his soulmate, and also a werewolf, but forgets to mention he already has someone in his life?!

Even being without him today makes me miss him. It must be that damned mate bond. A mate bond that I have with a freaking werewolf. Oh, and in case that wasn't batshit crazy enough, I'm a werewolf?!

I can't really deny he's a werewolf; I saw it with my own eyes. I felt his fur between my fingers. The thought sends similar tingles through my body. *Dammit, stop thinking about him.* As far as me being a werewolf, though, the jury is still out on that one. I need more proof.

My Pucking Mate

I'm sorry you lost them. They must have been amazing people to have raised such an amazing young woman.

He's an awfully smooth talker.

Do you have all these lines written down somewhere?

No my darling. I come from a different ...how can I put it...let's just say for now that I was raised differently so I sometimes communicate a little differently.

I guess I can understand that since I also have grown up totally different that most of the population.

Ok well are you busy? I was thinking we could ask each other a ton of questions and get to know each other.

If I'm being honest, I came here just wanting a normal college experience. I wasn't expecting a soulmate and new identity.

I'm not against having one, just give me time to let all this sink in, ok?

I'm headed into a team meeting right now, but how about a texting date? I can understand how you feel, and we'll take this at whatever pace you need. I'm not going anywhere.

That sounds fun, what time?

Thank you for understanding Roman.

4pm?

Talk to you then.

25
ROMAN

How am I supposed to focus on hockey, or anything else for that matter, ever again?

All I want to do is run to my mate and hold her; I want to learn everything about her that Slate wasn't able to dig up. Hell, just listen to her speak.

Walking into this team meeting is the second-to-last thing I want to be doing. The last thing I want to do is go to the two away games we have and be that far away from her.

I'm glad she took the text well and didn't even question where I got her number. That's a conversation for a later date. It's not that I won't tell her; I'll tell her everything. Just not yet. I don't want her to freak out and run. I'll tell her everything after she falls in love with me.

The information from Slate was helpful, though. I didn't actually read the information specifically about her because I really would like to learn that stuff from her. I mostly read up on her parents. They were some of the best photojournalists the world has ever seen. They received countless awards for their work throughout the years, and after looking at some of it myself, I'd have to agree. The shots they captured were breathtaking. There were even a couple cute pictures of her with them on their assignments. What a way to grow up—traveling the world and seeing animals and things most people only dream of.

But who were they really? Were they wolves? If not, how did they end up with a werewolf as a daughter? Slate still hasn't been able to locate any records of her birth. She just appeared. No birth records. No adoption records. Nothing. Digging deeper, we couldn't find the records for her parents either. It gets weirder. At least Leera has medical records. They don't. Not one. Ever.

Shaking my head, I don't have time to dwell further, though, because it's time for the team meeting.

After hours of listening to Coach drone on about plays we all know like the back of our hands and how every game counts if we want to make it to the playoffs this year, we're finally out of there. Perfect timing too. I have an hour and a half to get cleaned up and ready for a digital date with my little lady.

Unfortunately, I'm so lost in thought that I don't even notice India standing in basically a battle stance waiting for me outside the arena. I turn to glare at Benny when he pipes up, *that will teach you to keep your walls up. I tried to tell you.* I can hear the smug smirk on his face right now and I have half a mind to smack it off.

"Leave India," I say, my voice leaving little room for argument. She falters for just a moment before regaining her I'm-gonna-throw-a-bitch-fit posture.

"I'm not leaving until you tell me what's going on! I thought we were finally making progress and now you're using the goon squad to avoid me. That's not going to work for me, Roman. I will be your queen so it's time you get used to me," she finishes strong but when she sees the look on my face her facade slips again.

"I'm not having this discussion right now, and I'm sure as fuck not having it here," I say, baring my teeth and trudging past her to our SUV.

All my men pile into the vehicle and just sit in silence. "Out with it." I snap as I turn the car on. "I know at least one of you dicks has something to say. Go ahead and spit it out."

Andrei is the one who speaks up, "Wouldn't it be easier just to tell her about Leera? Tell her that she won't be anyone's queen? I'd love to watch it knock her off that fucking pedestal."

"I thought about it, but no, I don't think so. I don't trust India. I also don't want it to get back to my father yet, since they're apparently buddies now. And this whole business with the King . . ." Scrubbing one hand down my face and steering the SUV with the other.

"I want Leera to be comfortable and secure before we do anything to taint it."

"And what if the King no longer chooses you without India? Or vice versa, he still wants you to be king, making Leera a queen?" Slate asks, always two steps ahead of everyone.

I sigh and feign at the thought, but I already know the answer without a shadow of a doubt, "I can only hope the King can see what the result would be with India as the queen, with or without a king. As far as Leera and I, if that's in the cards we'll address it at that time, and if she doesn't wish to rule, then they'll have to figure it out. Leera is my life now. Before everything. I'll follow her wherever she needs or wants to go. I know we haven't really gotten to talk about it, so I understand if you all can't do that, but I won't live a moment doing anything other than making her happy."

Eris gags and Dolos joins in, "We don't want a mate if this is what it does to us." They joke at my sincerity, but we all know that's a lie.

With the longevity of our lives, every werewolf's sole purpose is to find their mate. Without them, they will always feel a level of emptiness. Once that emptiness has been filled, it usually kills us if it's lost. It almost killed me. And when it didn't, I nearly finished the job. I would have without these men. I'm even more thankful for them now that I have her. If I had given it all up then, I wouldn't have this chance now.

Without hesitation, Benny speaks up, "Wherever you go, I go, Boss. Always." And I know he means it. We've been together for almost three-quarters of a millennium. I can't even begin to imagine a life where he's not here.

The rest of the men somber themselves and nod in agreement. *Always.* They all announce themselves as one. Because though we are six very different men, we are a unit—a family. I can't wait to add our Luna to the mix.

We drive the rest of the way home in comfortable silence.

As we all pile out of the SUV, everyone makes their way to the elevators up to the main floor. I'm still grabbing my things out of the car when Andrei comes around the back.

"Roman, I want you to know that even though I haven't been around as long as the rest of the men, you have my full respect and loyalty. You are my Alpha, and I will stay by your side for as long as you'll allow." I think he's done, but he continues, "and for what it's worth, I think you'll make a great king." Before I can respond, he's walking away.

Replaying the interaction through my mind, it feels like he knows something that I don't know, but I shake it off as my irritation with recent events have been making me read too far into things.

It's three-thirty and I'm trying to decide what proper etiquette is for a texting date.

Can I text her a few minutes early, or do I wait until four o'clock on the dot?

Is it okay to stay in my lounge clothes, or should I put on presentable clothes just in case?

Part of me wants to ask her to dinner, but I don't want to push her. *ARG why does this have to be so complicated?!* If she was raised knowing she was a werewolf, all this mate stuff would be so much easier. You acknowledge your mate, spend pretty much all your time together, seal the mate bond and live happily ever after, or at least that's how it's told to young wolves who have never felt the pain of losing their mate.

It's not that I ever truly stopped thinking of Imogen, but she's been on my mind more often lately. I know they share a soul but sometimes my conscience eats at me, and I feel like I'm betraying her. Betraying her memory. Betraying what we had. I have to remind myself that the Goddess is giving her back to me for a reason, and I will not squander this rare opportunity.

I've been trying my best not to compare them, but that's also becoming more difficult. Their features are similar in the way they look soft and are too kind for the world we live in. Imogen was all dark colors, though, while Leera is lighter. Imogen had brown hair and brown eyes. Leera's hair is silver, and she has blue eyes. They seem to share a love for flowers, though, so I'm already well versed in the world of horticulture.

With only a few minutes to spare, I decide I'd rather be early.

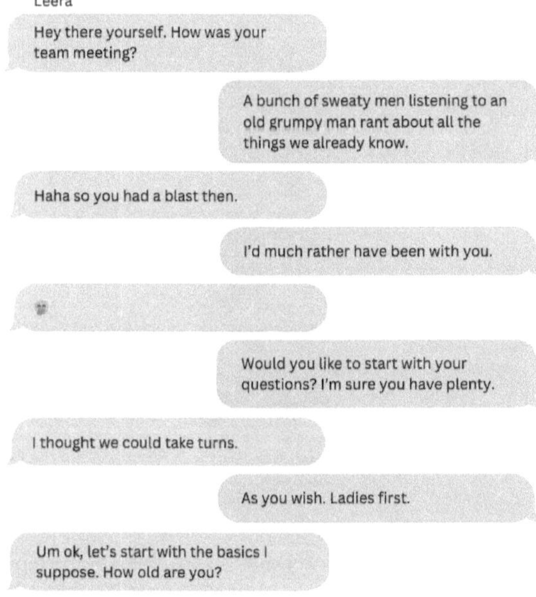

The immediate texting bubbles lift my spirits even higher. *She was waiting for me.*

Shit. I didn't think this through.

Oh. Um, well, we didn't get a chance to talk about that stuff. Werewolves are immortal, mostly.

OMG.

No way!

Really?!

Yes.

So that means I'm...?

Yes.

Wow.

Ok I'm ready for it.

How old are you?

...

Promise you won't, what's it called... ... ghost me?

I would never.

Pinky promise.

Seven hundred and thirteen years old.

Oh. Wow. Do all seven hundred and thirteen year old wolves look as good as you?

At least she thinks I look good. I chuckle to myself. *Maybe this won't be so bad.*

Crap I need an unsend button.

> How old are you?

Eighteen, to my knowledge. Lol.

> Oh. I know that sounds bad to humans. I'm sorry.

Why on earth would you apologize for your age?

I have a feeling that's not how fate works.

What age is your body compared to humans? I guess I could have looked it up on your hockey stats...

> I don't mind. I claim to be twenty-five so I'm not too young but still have lots of time left in my hockey career.

So when you're supposed to be getting older what do you do?

> We usually just go off the grid. Some go into hiding for fifty years, or so. Some just move to another country and start over. We have options.

That's kind of amazing.

Oops I got carried away and asked two questions. Your turn!

> What's your favorite color, food, and flower?

Back to basics. I like it.

Pink.

Probably Pizza but I'm a self proclaimed foodie, so I love lots of foods.

Um I can't choose a single favorite flower. They all smell different and they're so colorful and beautiful.

What's your favorite color?

That's easy, it used to be maroon but now it's . . .

It's a tie between silver and ice blue.

And how long have those been your favorite colors?

A couple weeks now.

Lol ok Prince Charming.

Your turn.

I feel like you probably have way more questions than I do.

How are you feeling about all of this?

Well I'm kinda bouncing back and forth between wondering who the hell I really am, inexplicably missing you, and in a whole lot of awe.

Also can't wait to learn more about my wolf and meet her.

My wolf and I can't wait to meet her either.

Can I ask you something crazy?

Can I ask you something crazy first?

You can ask me anything, whenever you need to. I truly mean that.

I'm getting hungry, do you maybe have time to meet up for dinner and we can keep talking, in person?

If not that's totally fine too.

Dress comfortably, I'm on my way!

26

Leera

He said dress comfortably, but what level of comfy are we going for here? Athletic-comfy? Absolute home-comfy? Cute-comfy? Not actually comfy but just public appropriate casual? UGH!

I settle on a happy medium and wear my grey, flared leggings, a hot pink, cropped tee, and a powder pink, oversized crewneck sweatshirt. I finish off the look with little messy space buns and my white tennis shoes and I'll be ready for anything.

I'm finishing up an assignment when there's a knock on the door. I scurry to the door to open it as fast as I can. *Holy shit. I wonder how long it will take for the sight of him to stop knocking the air from my lungs.*

As I swing open the door, I can't help but take inventory of the man in front of me. Dark grey jogger sweats and a black V-neck T-shirt that barely contains his arms. The T-shirt is also failing miserably at hiding how incredibly toned his body is. I'm not talking lean-ripped; I'm talking THICK and ripped. He's built like a tree trunk but with muscles. Does that even make sense? Even his hair is a bit disheveled and *OMG* he's holding a bouquet of rainbow daises.

"See something you like?" he asks with a breathtaking smile on his face, but I still can't make words.

"These are for you." He chuckles. "I got you a vase for these; I didn't think to ask last time because it was a surprise, so I decided to just be prepared this time."

Finally coming to my senses, I accept the adorable flowers. "Thank you so much; these are perfect. Yeah, I didn't have one, but now my little rose can live with the daisies," I say, rearranging them and discarding the solo cup.

"This is really so sweet. Thank you, Roman," I say, trying not to blush all over.

"You're very welcome. I've never courted or dated anyone, so you'll have to tell me if I do something wrong," he says with absolute certainty as I just stare and nod for a minute.

"Welp, what are we up to?" I ask.

"I hope you don't mind staying in; I have a surprise for you back at my place. Good surprises only this time, I promise."

Nodding, I collect my things. "That sounds wonderful."

As I'm locking the door to our dorm, my watch goes off. "Oh, crap, let me take my vitamins real quick. I swear, without my alarm, I'd forget them," I say with a giggle. "You can come back in with me so you don't get attacked by a crazed fan or something in the hall. Speaking of, you're lucky you haven't been spotted yet. You'll be signing autographs forever when it happens."

The sound of his half-laughter shoots through me. I wonder what his real, full-body laugh sounds like. I bet it sounds like magic.

As I'm grabbing my vitamins out of the cabinet, I manage to knock the old bottle off the shelf, and it rolls across the floor to Roman's feet. He bends to pick it up for me, but there's a borderline scary look on his face.

"What is this?" he asks, his voice low and dangerous, like the day I met him.

"Um, you're going to think I'm crazy," I say with a half-hearted laugh.

"Better than what's going through my mind right now. What is this?"

"Okay, um, I don't know what you think it is but it's just the last bottle, and the last multivitamin that my dad bought me before I lost them. It's just a weird little thing I couldn't part with. Why are you looking at it like that?" I ask, the anxiety now rising in my chest.

"Do you know what this is?"

"Is that a trick question? I just told you what it is."

"This is not a vitamin of any kind."

"What?" I whisper. "Wh-what is it?"

"Leera, this is poison."

The anxiety is immediately extinguished while shock and confusion make themselves at home in my body.

"Th-that can't be true. Those are the vitamins I took my whole life. I'm sorry, Roman, but you have to be mistaken."

"Leera, look at me. This is a poison called wolfsbane. In small doses, it prevents someone's wolf from surfacing. In large doses it can be fatal."

The room is spinning, and I can't get enough oxygen to my lungs. I'm just staring at Roman, but I can see the gears turning in his mind when he says, "How long have you been out of vitamins?"

"J-just a couple weeks. I-I couldn't find them online any-where, so I j-just bought a popular multivitamin."

"Your parents knew," he says so quietly I'm sure he's actual-ly talking to himself before he lifts his head and stares directly at me, "your parents knew."

"My parents knew wh . . ." I trail off when my mind finally catches up with Roman's, and I can no longer control my body as I crumble to the floor.

"My parents knew." I want to scream at him and call him a liar. I want to tell him my parents would never do that to me, but I feel the truth in my soul. How the hell else would I live my entire life without knowing I'm a werewolf?

I'm the one talking to myself now, "My parents knew I was a wolf and they poisoned me my whole life. No. That's not possible. My parents loved me. They would never p-poison me." I'm trying so hard to take deep gulps of oxygen but it's just not enough.

"My parents knew I was a wolf and they poisoned me my whole life!" I'm yelling now. "Who were they? Were they hu-man? Were they wolves?"

I feel the spiraling fear seeping into my bones when a warm body nearly completely envelops me in an embrace that I can feel from my toes to my soul. I've never been touched like this by anyone, let alone a giant man. My brain is telling me it's a little fast but my body and my heart wish he'd never let go.

"Shhhhh sunshine, it's going to be okay. No matter what we find, or what happens for the rest of my life, I promise, it will be okay. I'll make sure of it," he says while rubbing my back and soothing the panic from my body.

I feel that strange feeling under my skin again.

"Roman," I gasp.

He looks at me with concern and compassion.

"I thought I felt something under my skin. It was a calm feeling, like when a cat rubs against your legs."

He squeezes me tighter, and I'm pretty sure I would die happy if we stayed just like this for the rest of my existence.

"That's your wolf. She's either trying to calm you, or she's trying to nuzzle me and my wolf. Which means she's definitely waking up from the sedation she's been under for, well, forever.

It's such a surreal thing to realize your body is not just your own and it's also not the only form you possess.

I don't know how long we sit like that, not saying a word, just holding each other and soaking each other in when I speak up, "Hey Roman?"

"Yeah, Sweetheart?"

"Can we pretend this didn't happen for a little while and go about our evening? We can figure this out later, can't we? I'm hungry," I pout.

It's not just the hunger that needs to postpone this moment. This is just too much information. I can't wait to meet my wolf, but after the pain from last time, it's also terrifying.

I can't wait to meet you, but I'm scared. I'm sure werewolves are supposed to be strong and brave, but you'll have to be patient with me. I tell my wolf, hoping she can hear me. Last time there was no response, but this time I feel the same calming brush under my skin. I allow myself a small smile at her compassion.

"Of course we can," and just like that, he's pulling me to my feet and towards the door. "Is it okay with you if I take this bottle to Jeanine—the healer—to look at?"

I just nod because I still can't believe I might have been poisoned my whole life. If this is true, my parents poisoned me my entire life. The only people I had in the whole world. The people I thought about every day. The people who knew I was a werewolf and never told me. Did I even know them? I know they loved me, though . . . right?

When we pull up to their home, I'm plagued by flashbacks of my last visit. I don't think I'll ever get used to going to this giant townhouse.

I really hope *she* doesn't show up again.

As if sensing my concern, Roman says, "She won't be here. I promise."

"Are we going to be talking about that?" I ask timidly.

"Yes, let's go up and let me surprise you. Then we can return to our conversation, and you can keep asking me anything you'd like."

Again, I just nod and allow him to lead me inside.

As we walk through the door, we stand in the entry for a moment while he discards his wallet onto the side table and adds his keys to a hook with an R above it. I giggle when I notice they all have their own key and someone has put them on the wall in order to say, B E A R D S. "That was Benny," Roman says with a huff of a laugh.

As we enter their living space, I still can't fully comprehend the enormity of it. Everything is high ceilings, a full wall of windows, an open floor plan, and the works, and it's totally man-cave-esque. I didn't even notice how beautiful it was in here. Last time I was here, I was whisked in while in terrible pain. Then on my way out, we had the incident with India. I never really got to just look around.

The living room is to my right and it's kind of set up like a pit. You have to take two steps down to get into the space, then the entire left edge of the recessed room is a giant black suede couch. There are ottomans throughout the room, in case someone wants to kick their feet up or use it as a table. The only other thing in the room is the largest television I've ever seen. Can it even be considered a TV at that size? It looks like a movie theater screen. I wonder how they can even see what they're watching with all the windows. Seriously, the entire far wall ahead of me is nothing but a giant window overlooking the small city below.

To the left of the living room is a massive, white marble kitchen island with barstools wrapped around it, making it look like some kind of gateway to a kitchen straight out of a dream kitchen magazine. I can't see much of it from here, but there are cabinets and doors all over.

Further to the left is a hallway, a sleek open staircase, and the stairs we used to get to the rooftop.

Benny reaches us first, bringing me back to the moment. He's smiling and bouncing on the balls of his feet. "Hey, Leera! Welcome back! We'll make ourselves scarce, but just holler if you need us to gang up on the old grump, yeah?" He takes off just in time to avoid what would have been a smack to the back of his head from Roman, making me giggle again.

The twins pass us next heading out the door, saluting Roman as they go. "They're on security detail tonight to ensure there are no uninvited guests."

I turn to Roman raising my eyebrow and asking, "Why are they on security duty? Don't you have actual security guards or something?"

"Of course we do, but she's gotten past them before, and I want to be certain it's not a problem."

Slate is perched on the barstool at the end of the island, focused on a tablet in his hands, but he lifts an arm up in an awkward, backward wave.

Andrei is sitting on one of the ottomans in the living room, feigning casual indifference, but there's a strange look on his face, and his body language is tense. I feel a different kind of tug towards him that I still don't understand. Seeming to notice it as well, he looks in our direction, and we make eye contact for only a moment before he quickly bolts from the room, leaving me feeling like I did something wrong. *Werewolves are weird.*

Roman is still leading me through their home while my thoughts wander to all I've learned today. We reach the door to the roof, and my excitement returns.

"You seemed to really enjoy it up here the other night, so I added a few things," he tells me almost sheepishly. I've never seen such a giant, gorgeous man look bashful, but I kind of love it.

I'm probably smiling like an idiot while he practically drags me up the stairs. He stops on the top steps and spins around so fast that it causes me to fumble for the handrails. "Will you . . . will you close your eyes?" he asks. I smile and nod, closing my eyes and leaving the smile on my face.

In the darkness, I hear him open the door. He grabs my hand and slowly pulls me onto the roof, taking one, two, three, four steps towards the center, I think.

He comes to stand behind me, wrapping his arms around my waist. The intimate gesture startles me at first. Once I feel the tingles of our contact, I relax into him, and it releases a whole bunch of butterflies in my belly.

He leans in a bit, resting his chin on top of my head, and all the butterflies lose their minds.

"Open your eyes," he whispers with his smooth yet gravelly voice, causing a wave of goosebumps to rush down my arms.

I slowly follow his instructions, not at all prepared for the sight before me.

I gasp in shock, both hands flying up to cover my mouth while my body whips around to face him.

"You did all this for me?" I ask with tears in my eyes.

"I did. The guys helped, but yes, it's for you."

I turn back around to take in every single detail and commit it to memory.

The rooftop has been transformed into a magical escape from reality. There are twinkle lights strung all over the place. There's a giant white screen by the outdoor furniture for watching movies. There's a pizza buffet and a coffee bar.

Their townhouse is in the perfect neighborhood, on top of a hill, just outside of town. There are other houses, but they each have their own giant lot. If I threw a rock, I don't think I could hit another house. Overlooking one side of the roof are little lights scattered against the dark expanse of land, showing the small city below. Off the other side of the roof is all wooded acreage. *I bet the men let their wolves loose in there.*

"Roman . . . this . . . it's too much." I say, shaking my head, still in awe of all of the thought he put into this.

This is crazy.

"Nonsense. I found it on the Pinterest," he says as he drops a tiny kiss onto my forehead, and I melt into a puddle at his feet.

"Do you like it? Did I do it wrong?"

Slowly shaking my head, "This is perfect," I say quietly.

He leads me over to where the pizza and coffee are all spread out for us to enjoy. There's also hot cocoa, which I hadn't noticed before.

"I love food and all, but this is a lot, even for me," I joke.

"Whatever we don't eat won't last the night. Depending on the day, one of the guys could eat all this on their own," he says with a small chuckle.

He hands me a plate and picks up one for himself. We both pile them with pizza and sweets and carry them over to the large couch. After setting our plates on the table, we head back for drinks.

"I know the other night you didn't want coffee because it would keep you up, so I made decaf. That way, if you really wanted the coffee, you could have it."

This man thought of everything, and it's definitely not helping the butterfly situation in my middle.

"That was so incredibly sweet of you to remember. Thank you," I say lightly as I try to keep the tears from reaching my eyes. Failing miserably, I lower my chin so he doesn't see.

Of course he notices, though. He grabs my chin with just his thumb and pointer finger and slowly lifts my eyes back up to his. "What did I do? Are you okay?" he asks, his voice full of concern, one green eye, and one blue, searching mine.

"Absolutely nothing. Everything is more perfect than I ever could have imagined. I guess I'm just a little overwhelmed. I only ever had my parents, and they loved me, but it's like, even though they loved me completely and I was always happy, I don't know . . . it just . . . it just feels like I never actually knew what being cared for by someone else could feel like. I didn't feel this overwhelming sense of . . ."

How do I explain that I thought I was happy and loved my whole life, but now I don't feel like I know anything? When Roman holds me, hell, when he touches me, the warmth and the *rightness* that I feel . . . . . .what do I call that? It's way too soon to say or even think about the L-word, but even this feels like *more.*

"And now, with my vitamins, I feel like I don't know anything anymore. I wasn't prepared for this much emotion."

His eyes soften, and his body relaxes, like he was worried that I was about to run.

"I guess if you want, I could tone it down some more and we could slow down to a glacial speed," he replies with a cocky grin on his face, causing me to giggle a little through my tears.

"You'll do no such thing. I'm already loving this new level of pampering you've introduced me to." I say with a smirk of my own.

We finish making our drinks in comfortable silence and make our way back to our food. We sit, and I can't help but marvel at the view, the company, and the twinkling lights.

Am I in some kind of coma where I'm living out some fantasy rom-com? Was I hit by a car or something?

"So," he begins hesitantly, swallowing his pizza in a dramatic gulp. "Ask me all your questions. I'll answer them all. Complete honesty."

Nodding, I also swallow my pizza and set down my plate of food, dusting off my hands. I take a deep breath. "Let's start with her. What was that the other night? What are you to her?" I hate feeling vulnerable over someone I barely know, but I don't have control over my feelings towards him.

"Okay, I promised you complete honesty, so please just hear me out. Let me get it all out, and if there are more questions, you can ask them, and as long as I know the answer, I'll provide it. Okay?"

"Okay," I say, feeling small and skeptical.

"Her name is India. Her father and mine have been friends since their youth. They both came from upper-class families, but where her father grew to become our king's advisor, my father never obtained a title. I rose to power to be the commander of the king's army. For whatever reason, our fathers always wanted us to be together, but I didn't want any part of it. I found my mate. Her name was Imogen, and all I wanted was a life with her. She wasn't noble or high-class, and that infuriated my father. She was born in the village, and she had the most amazing heart. We didn't care what anyone said. So, we made ourselves a home and were starting our lives together . . ." He pauses, and I'm not sure I'm ready for what he has to tell me if it hurts him like this.

"Roman, you don't have t—" I start.

"Yes, I do. You need to know everything. You need to know who I am and why I am the way I am sometimes. The sooner, the better."

I just nod and take his giant hand in mine.

"We were just starting our lives together. She was pregnant with our first child. She was crazy; she wanted as many kids as we could have. I was called away for an emergency involving the army one day. I promised I'd be right back. I wasn't even gone four hours when I knew something was wrong and raced home. She was murdered."

I'm openly crying now. This man lost his mate and his child. "Did you find out who did it? Why they did it?" I ask quietly through my sniffles.

He lowers his head and shakes it. I think that's all the response he'll give when he speaks. "I never found anything. None of my men did either. The only people who ever even disliked her were my father and Khaos' father. Even though they disliked her, I never suspected them capable of murdering her without proof of any kind."

"So that's why when I showed up . . ."

It's his turn to just nod.

He takes a deep breath and begins again. "Losing your mate is one of the most painful things any paranormal or supernatural being can go through. They're the other half of your soul. So after a pair has bonded, their souls are merged into only one soul, as the Goddess intended. Losing one means your soul is then ripped in half, and it doesn't ever really heal again. Most shifters follow their mate in death. My rage, and Benny, were the only things that kept me alive. I'm glad I got through all of that before I found you."

He looks at me like I hung the moon with my bare hands. "I fear you would have thought me a barbaric monster and never given me a chance. Hell, I was a monster. But I came out on the other side. I got myself together. My men and I started making plans. But apparently we weren't the only ones. My father and India's father were making plans of their own. When I had finally healed, as much as one could, they advised me that India and I were to be wed. I let them know of my plans for America and hockey and what me and my men wanted to do for a time. They said I could have my fun, but when I was done, I would have to marry her. I didn't care anymore. I didn't have a reason to fight them other than I would never be able to love her."

He sighs while I just stare at him. Judging by the look on his face, I'm really not going to like what he says next.

"What is it?" I ask, not really wanting to know anymore but knowing I have to nonetheless.

"India and I are still betrothed and . . . I just recently found out the king wants her and me to take the throne. I haven't spoken to my father about it anymore, so I can only assume that I was chosen for my work with the army of werewolves. I've been with the King on many occasions to take care of our people. With India, it would have to be her upbringing. Though she wasn't royal, being the daughter of the king's advisor, she had been taught by royal tutors. But all of that was before this," he says, waving his hands between us as he rushes to continue speaking. "I don't care who it upsets; I will not marry her, and I will not take the throne beside her. Leera, you are my everything. I know that doesn't make sense to you yet, but it will. I can hardly breathe when you're not within reach. I will move the mountains and oceans for you if I must. But please trust me when I say there has never and will never be anything of measure between her and me."

It's his turn to drop his head as he tangles his fingers in his hair with the hand I'm not holding.

"Have you told her? Does she know it's over?" I ask, but the look on his face is all the answer I need.

27
ROMAN

How do I explain this to her without her misunderstanding me? Please don't let her hate me.

She jumps to her feet, fire in her icy eyes. "So you're sitting here claiming me, but you're also still supposed to marry another woman?!" she nearly shouts as she begins pacing a small space just in front of me.

"You promised to listen to everything. I'm not finished yet," I try to sound strong and sure, but it comes out as more of a beg.

She slowly turns her narrowed eyes on me before reclaiming her seat next to me, crossing her arms over her chest, not retaking my hand.

"I haven't told her yet for a few reasons. Most importantly because I don't trust her. She isn't used to not getting her way, and I don't know how she will react. I also don't care for or trust my father. They seem to have built some kind of relationship over time. It wasn't a potential concern before you entered my life, so I didn't care."

Slate, before I forget, I need you to do some digging. Are there any connections you can find between India and my father?

You got it, boss.

"I'm not ready for him to know about you either. As selfish as it is, I want you to myself for a while. I'm keeping her away, and I haven't touched her since I found you. I swear it." I finish and wait for what feels like an eternity before she says anything.

"So you and her . . . how long have you been *together?*" she asks, twisting the words together to sound like a curse.

"We have been betrothed and occasionally physical for a little over a hundred years. Never anything permanent. In passing when she happens across this part of the world through her travels," I say with guilt.

She seems to turn green at the thought, and I don't know what to say or do.

"Please don't hate me." I wish so quietly that she barely hears me.

"Oh Roman . . . shit. I don't hate you. But, fuck! How am I supposed to feel? I'm up against a woman you have been with for over a hundred years?! It doesn't matter how seriously you took it. It's still a relationship. In the human world, it's called being engaged, which makes me the homewrecker!" She's pacing back and forth now, and it's killing me not to reach out and hold her.

"Leera, I swear to you. I will make this right, but there is absolutely no fucking contest here. You are my *mate.* Even if we had already married, if I were already a fucking king, I would drop everything and be yours. That's how this works. Our souls were made to exist together. While uncommon, it does happen where someone finds their fated mate after starting a life, sometimes a family. That's why most prefer to wait for their mate."

"It's not just that. I just hate the thought of you with her.

Especially . . . *physically.* I um . . ." She falters and turns away from me.

"What is it?" I ask, softly reaching for her hand and turning her back around to face me.

"I um . . . I've never . . . I've never been with anyone. I've n-never done anything." Another long pause, but I wait this one out in shock. "My only experiences with love come from my parents. I never had friends, and definitely never a boyfriend. I obviously never expected to find a mate. I thought I'd have some mild college experience, but now I feel like I've been thrown in the deep end without knowing how to swim."

I release the breath I didn't realize I'd been holding and scrub my hands across my face, trying to keep my composure. She would not appreciate it if I smiled right now. I'm shocked only because I've seen how these humans act, but the thought of her being mine in every way makes blood rush to my dick. *It is not the time for this.* But my wolf and body do not agree. *Pull yourself together.*

"No matter what we are, Leera, everything that happens from this day forward is only what you want. We'll take everything as slow as you want. Thank you for telling me, though. I wish I could erase my past so that it was only you and Imogen, but I can't. I hope you can forgive me."

"There's nothing to forgive. I think I'm just feeling a little overwhelmed and insecure. She's so sophisticated and beautiful. How could you even want me when—"

"Don't ever think so little of yourself. She is a beautiful woman by many standards, but she's never been that for me. I've never felt a genuine connection to her. Even when we've been *together* there was nothing romantic about it. I'm ashamed to admit it, but I've really only been existing. It's why I didn't fight the betrothal. It was only recently that I was even trying to find my way out of the marriage arrangement. It's like my heart knew you were coming for me."

That seems to relax her a smidge.

"Okay," she says as she releases a sigh that seems to have taken a weight off her shoulders.

"What else?" I ask. "Even if it's not pretty, I'll tell you everything."

"Why haven't I met my wolf since I'm out of my . . . vitamins? Shouldn't I be able to shift now?"

"We'll need to speak to the healer about it. You were poisoned your whole life; it could have lingering effects."

She nods, then says, "I meant it when I said I'd like you to work for this. I'd still like a semi-normal experience here. I feel the tug between us. I'm obviously drawn to you and feel more than I ever thought possible, but I'd still really like to have the experience of dating and such. I'm sure that sounds silly."

I finally allow myself to smile. *I've still got her.* She feels all of this with me.

"You got it. I'm all in. I've never had the full human experience either. It will be something that is only ours," I say, gathering both of her hands in mine. "All we have is time. No matter what it takes, no matter how long it takes, I'm yours."

The blush that starts on the apples of her cheeks and spreads down her neck is intoxicating.

"I uh . . . I think that's all of my questions for now. Can we go back to our snacks? Did you still want to watch a movie?"

"Yes," I say, kissing her on top of her head as I stand to get more food now that I can stomach it. "You can still ask me anything when you're ready. What do you want to watch?" I ask over my shoulder.

I turn back to the couch with food in hand, and I'm struck by the adorable look on her face. Her nose is scrunched up, and she's tapping her chin while she thinks. I make a mental note to ask her as many questions as I can, just to see this look on her face.

"Well that depends," she says, "do we watch something fun or mushy or scary?"

"Anything you want."

"You say that like that makes it easy to decide. Do you know how many good movies there are? Of course you do; you've probably seen them all."

Goddess she's cute when she's all worked up. I like when she rambles. She just lets her thoughts flow straight out of her mouth. It's hard to find such brutally honest people. *Taking her and Benny out in public together will be fun, I'm sure.*

"Okay, Roman, lesson number one, I'm incredibly indecisive about almost all things. I will need to be given options, or you will need to choose because it's just too much." She finishes with a small giggle, which I match with a low chuckle of my own.

"Got it. How about this? When I ask you what's one of your favorite movies, what's the first movie that comes to mind?"

I should have been afraid of the smile that spread across her face, but I couldn't bring myself to care about whatever media torture she imposed.

"You don't want to watch that," she says as she makes her way back to the buffet of pizza, with a mesmerizing sway to her hips.

She comes back with a plate full, and I love that she isn't one of those women who starves themselves or won't eat on a date. She plops onto the couch so close to me that I find myself wishing she would have landed on my lap. Growling at the image, I shake it from my mind. *Slow down. She needs time.*

She notices and quirks her brow at me before returning to the conversation at hand. "Twilight," she announces proudly as she takes a bite of her pizza and nearly moans. My brain is firing in too many directions. It takes me a moment to process what she's said when I'm groaning for another reason.

"Alright, but don't tell the guys." I wink. "I'll never hear the end of it."

She smiles and nods, moving her pinched thumb and pointer finger across her lips and pretending to lock them and throw away a key.

I chuckle and pull up the app on the tablet to play the movie through the projector.

"It's so beautiful up here," she mumbles around her mouth, stuffed with pizza, as she stares out at the lights of the city.

"It's never been more beautiful," I reply, staring only at her.

28
Leera

Waking up to Zoey crashing around our dorm room is my new normal. She's basically my alarm clock at this point. I have an alarm set, but she takes longer to get ready in the morning, so hers goes off earlier, in turn waking me with her crashing around. It was a little frustrating at first, but now it's just another Tuesday.

"Good morning!" I singsong to her. I'm a morning person, and she most definitely is NOT, so it always makes me giggle.

My phone goes off, and the smile that takes over my face is a bit ridiculous, but I know it's him. No one else texts me in the morning. Very few people even have my number.

My Pucking Mate

Good Morning Beautiful.

Good Morning yourself.

I hate that we have away games all week and I won't get to see you again until Saturday.

Ugh, I forgot about that. *This is going to suck; I think I already miss him. I'm so screwed.*

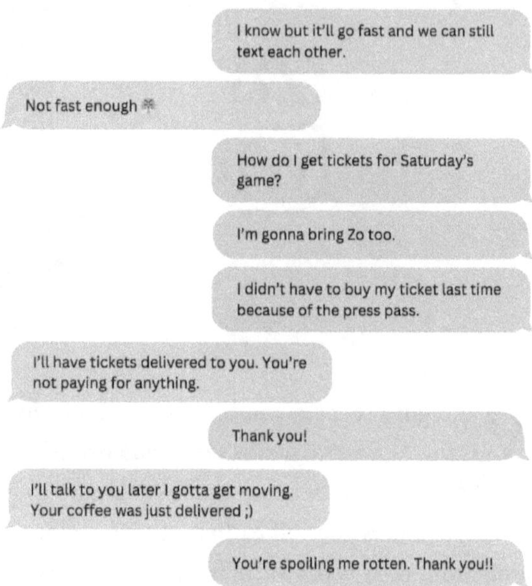

Just as my feet hit the floor to go grab my coffee, Zoey opens the door and laughs. "You're not going to believe this," she says, turning towards me and crossing her arms over her chest.

I throw on my robe and rush to the door, releasing a small gasp.

Roman did not just have coffee delivered. There's a bouquet of lily flowers of all colors with my coffee, all sitting on a cute little hallway table. I snatch the card out of the flowers first.

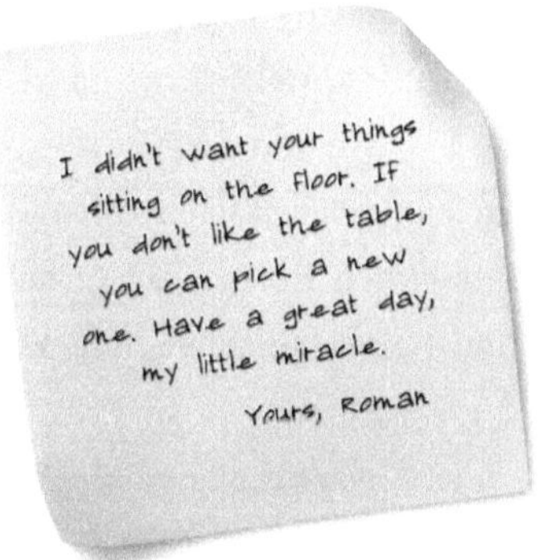

Clutching the card to my chest, I do a little twirl in the doorway, forgetting we live in a busy college dorm and people are already staring over the scene in the hallway.

Blushing furiously, I grab my coffee and flowers and scramble back into our room, slamming the door in my hurry.

Zoey is just staring at me, arms still crossed over her chest, "If he's going to bring so much attention to us, he could at least send me coffee too, my favorite is an iced caramel macchiato." If you didn't know her, you'd think she was irritated, but she's happy for me and just poking fun.

> OMG you caused a scene this morning but thank you again for everything! I love the table. The flowers are gorgeous! My coffee is delicious.

> Oh and Zoey says if you're going to continue to embarrass us, she would like some coffee too. Iced Caramel Macchiato.

I toss my phone on the bed and get ready for the day, not waiting for a response since he already told me he had to run.

The week carries on mostly without excitement. It's not the longest week ever, but it definitely didn't go by quickly.

I did feel a few . . . how do I explain it . . . stirrings? But it was so light, I don't know if it's her or my imagination. She doesn't seem as strong when Roman is not around. Maybe the bond helps to strengthen her, since we may have been poisoned my whole life.

Roman and I texted every day, but it's not the same as feeling the electricity between us when we're together.

It's finally Saturday, which means I'll get to see him tonight!

Last night, a delivery man came by with our tickets and a giant box with a big pink bow. We tore into that box so fast, it was comical. Nestled inside were two maroon jerseys for us to wear to the game!

Mine, of course, was Roman's name and number, while Zoey got a custom jersey with her name on it and a big zero-zero instead of one of the players numbers.

This man's thoughtfulness never ceases to amaze me. Of course I'd want his jersey, but he had one made for Zo so she would be comfortable.

We're getting ready for the game now, and I'm going with a bundled chic look because I didn't realize before how cold it gets in there. I'm wearing a pair of thick but cute black cargo joggers, with a T-shirt underneath my plain black hoodie. Then I added my jersey over everything so that it can be seen. Keeping my jersey unobstructed, I fixed my hair into the cutest silver space buns and added a little hair glitter for fun. I went with a super natural make-up look, just some mascara and a little blush, but Zoey wasn't having it. She took my liquid eyeliner pen and added a cute little number twenty-three to both my cheeks.

We stop in front of the mirror to assess our handiwork. We did good. We look adorable, and I can't wait to get to the game to see what he thinks, though I probably won't get to see him until after.

I don't think that I'll ever get used to the feeling of walking into the giant arena for these games. Fans are buzzing around everywhere. Some are buying Predators gear at the souvenir shops; some are buying food; and lots are buying alcohol. The energy is charged, and it just makes you feel ready to go! It's nothing like the electricity that runs through my body at his touch, but it's definitely a feeling all its own.

An employee helps us find our seats when I present our tickets at the door, and we both share a curious look. I immediately understand why when we finally make it to the VIP seating directly behind the team's bench. The employee fills us in on the benefits of these seats, which is insane, by the way; we get free food and drinks all night long. We don't even have to go get it; the employees will. And sitting this close to the action is going to be an unreal experience. I can't even think about how much money these cost. As soon as he walks away, Zoey and I clasp hands and squeal a little. This is really happening.

We get some looks from everyone around us. The girls look jealous and judgy. The men look at us like we're a piece of meat. The employees are the only ones who don't look at us weirdly.

We order some soda and chili dogs to have while we wait for the team to come out and warm up. We got here as soon as the doors opened, so we didn't miss anything, along with everyone else, apparently.

We've just finished our food when the lights dim and the music is cranked way up. There are lights flashing all over the place as the opening show begins to introduce the team. Everyone roars as each teammate skates onto the ice as their name is called. The roaring of the crowd gets louder and louder as the players are announced, and we haven't even reached the ones I know yet. When it's finally time to announce the starters, the arena erupts.

Each starter announced is another explosion of energy. Just when I think it can't possibly get any louder, Roman skates onto the ice. Not a soul in the arena remains seated. Men, women, and children alike all scream his name, jumping, clapping, stomping, and squealing. For just a moment, though, I don't hear any of it. When our eyes connect, it's just the two of us in the whole world.

He's supposed to skate around the ice, but he skates directly towards me and hops into the bench box. We haven't broken eye contact, but I'm no longer immune to the crowd. Especially now that they're focused on where he's going—right to me. He stops directly in front of me, takes off his gloves, places one hand over his heart, and one hand on the plexiglass barrier between us. Everyone's staring, and I can feel my face heating with blush, but I take a step closer and mimic his stance. Placing one hand on my heart and the other against the plexiglass where his lies. The cameras are on us now. I'm on the freaking jumbotron, and the crowd is in utter disarray.

This is crazy. Absolutely insane. But I can't find it in me to care. Sure, the whole world can see me now. But looking into his eyes in this very moment. I can't find a fuck to give about anyone else.

29
ROMAN

Having her here at my game is a high I've never experienced. Seeing her in my jersey made my heart beat irregularly for a few moments. Having that moment with her before the game started was stupid, but there was nothing I could do to stop myself.

Really think that was a good idea, Boss? You said you wanted to keep her under wraps for now, and you know that's already all over the TV and internet. Slate reminds me through our link.

It wasn't a good idea, but I wasn't thinking. It just happened. FUCK.

If I thought it was a bad idea before, I'm really kicking myself when I see who's glaring at me from across the rink.

FUCK! All men turn to me, ready to fight, just by the tone of my voice alone.

Barely moving, I tip my head in the direction of the problem.

Standing against the railing of the rink, with her hands on her hips and a scowl on her face, is India. And judging from the look of her, she just saw everything.

Shit, what do we do? asks Benny.

There's nothing we can do until after the game, so right now we play and we win, then we deal with this after.

They all offer a clipped nod as a response, and we finish our drills as the game is about to begin.

I can only hope that Leera doesn't see her.

I learned my lesson from the last home game about trying to split my focus between Leera and the game. This time, I give her little looks, but mostly I'm focusing on the game so we can get this shit over with and I can be with her.

We're up one to zero at the end of the first period. As the team stands to head to the locker room, I place my gloved hand on the barrier as Leera bashfully does the same.

I don't like her leaving my sight. I should have brought her a pack guard, but I wasn't thinking. When she's with me, she doesn't need a guard, but I won't be there with her during intermissions or immediately after the game.

Sighing, I know there's nothing I can do about it now, so I hurry into the locker room with the men to prepare for the next period.

30
Leera

I watch him skate towards the locker room, and I am finally cooling off. Between our moment before the game, watching him play, and then just now, him not leaving without acknowledging me, I've been all in a tizzy of emotions.

Zoey giggles next to me, "Girl, you got it bad!" and I can't even deny it. No wonder people swoon after athletes; when you know one of them is yours, it changes the game completely. Every time he was hit, I would gasp. Each time he had the puck, I was tangling my fingers together. And, oh my gosh, when he made that goal, I came unglued! I wonder if it will always feel like this.

The waiter comes by to see if we want anything. Since it's free, we definitely do! "I'll take a pretzel with cheese and, uh, whatever cola you carry." He just nods, finishes scribbling, and looks over to Zo. "I'll take the same!" And with that, he scurries away.

"Isn't this incredible?! Can you Imagine how much these seats cost?" She says it a little more loudly than I'm comfortable with.

All of a sudden, her whole body freezes for a microsecond before her eyes narrow viciously when I hear, "Of course you couldn't imagine or ever afford these seats."

Just the sound of her voice makes me want to claw her eyes out a little. I slowly turn to face her. "I have nothing to say to you, India. Anything you want to say, you can say to Roman," I say, turning back around without even waiting for her response.

I can't believe I'm having to deal with this. Has he talked to her yet?

"Well, considering you're the one gallivanting around in public with MY fiancé, I'd say I have the right to say whatever I want to you."

He apparently has NOT talked to her. Fuck.

The shock on Zoey's face is too much. I should have given her some kind of head's up on that whole situation, but I didn't think it would matter. I looked up so many of Roman's games, and they were never seen together at any of his games.

"I'm sorry, but you really need to talk to Roman. This is his conversation to have with you." I don't want to have a very public incident with India right now.

"See, that doesn't work for me. He's busy, and you're right here. So how about you go ahead and tell me what lines he fed you about the kind of relationship you two can have? Because you have no idea what you're getting yourself into, and I promise you can't handle it."

I swear, Zoey's jaw hits the ground for a moment before she looks like she's going to fly at India. I shake my head at her, silently asking her to let me handle this. I hate confrontation. I've never had to be mean to anyone in my whole life, but I need her to understand that I will not cower and I will not deal with her.

"Look, India, the last time I checked, you've never been seen at a game with him. No one has. And when anyone looks up Roman Razboinic, he's one of the nation's hottest bachelors. So make a scene and have a fit if that's what you want, but I'm not having this conversation with you, especially not here. You need to talk to Roman." I say it with as much confidence as I can muster.

Zoey is looking back and forth between us when India finally stomps off with a huff.

Needless to say, I spend the rest of intermission explaining their situation to Zo at the human level. She's not happy with me, and if I'm being honest, I'm not all too happy with myself. Or Roman. I knew he hadn't talked to her yet last week, but why wasn't some time this week a good time to tell her? I've just tried to pretend she doesn't exist, but she isn't wrong. I'm here in public with her fiancé. Whether the world knows about them or not, it still feels wrong. *Why hasn't he talked to her?*

I wasn't expecting the *huff* response from within, and it makes me smile for a moment.

The next period is about to begin, and I hate that she was able to make me feel like a slime ball—like I'm the other woman when it's not like that, even though it is. I am the other woman. All because Roman hasn't talked to her yet.

What if she talks to the press, and that's what I'm tagged as, for the world to see? I can't just yell, "He's my mate!" and everyone would be like, "Oh, right. Okay. That's fine then." That's not how things work.

This is not how this night was supposed to go.

31
ROMAN

Coming back to the ice to see Leera pretending not to be upset is not what I wanted to see. I don't even have to ask her what's wrong. I'm not stupid enough to believe India would leave her alone. I didn't think about this because India hasn't been to any of our games since our first season. She doesn't like all the people and smells, and she doesn't like hockey.

That just made me love hockey even more.

But now Leera is upset, and I don't even know exactly what happened.

Ohhh you fucked up. Eris whoops through the link, Dolos chuckling with him before Andrei rams him into the wall.

Everyone knock it off; we've got a game to win, so I can deal with this.

32
India

I can't believe this! That tiny little bitch that Benny was holding at the townhouse that night wasn't there for him at all. The fucking runt was there for Roman.

Who the fuck does he think he is?! Wait until Daddy hears about this. Daddy will tell Roman's father, and he's going to regret his trashy little side piece.

It's not like anything can come of it. He's marrying *me*. *I'll* be his queen. Not some little rodent human girl.

Maybe it's just some publicity stunt crap.

Whatever it is, I'll take care of it.

I WILL be Queen.

But first, I'm going to call my daddy and tell him about the entire awful ordeal.

33
ROMAN

We're wrapping up the last period now. We're up four to one, so we're really just letting the clock run out at this point. Luckily, India left some time during the second period.

Just one more minute of game time, and I can head to the locker rooms and get the fuck out of here with my girl. She doesn't look as upset as she did. She doesn't look as happy either, though, and that bothers me. I'm going to have to take care of all of this as soon as possible.

The game finally ends, and I make a beeline for my girl. Keeping up appearances, I place my hand against the barrier; she does the same, but the smile on her face is forced and fake. It's not lighting up the room like it was earlier, and it's my fault. My wolf is furious beneath my skin for hurting our mate's feelings, and I can't even blame him.

34
Leera

They won the game, and I'm trying to be excited, but the episode with India really just sucked all the good energy out of the evening. I was so excited to see him after the long week of away games.

"Hey, you okay?" Zoey asks.

"Yeah, sorry, my drama was a bit of a buzzkill."

"Pssh, it's okay. It's not your fault. I still can't believe all that. You sure he's really leaving her, and it wasn't just a line?" she asks, not understanding since I can't tell her we're mates. So I just nod.

"Well, I'm sure you guys have some talking to do, at least, so I'm gonna go ahead and head home. Text me if you need anything," she says while giving me a hug before she heads up the steps.

"Text me when you're home safe," I holler up the steps to her.

I sit alone for a little while before a strange, but familiar, man plops down next to me. At first, he looks kind of distracted or confused before he seems to try to figure me out. He's not an unattractive man at all. I mean, he's not Roman. They're built similar, but where Roman has lighter hair, blue and green eyes, and golden skin, this man seems sharper. His black hair is slicked back, and grey piercing eyes, with lighter skin and a face that's all hard angles.

I feel like I should be afraid of him, but I'm not. There's another one of those weird feelings that doesn't make any sense. Not the warm, fluttery, and electrical feelings I get with Roman. Something other. I don't know how to explain it. It's kind of like how I feel around Andrei.

I don't know how long we've been lost in thought, assessing one another, when I realize he looks even more confused now himself, all the cocky guy energy he sat down with has dissipated.

"Um, can I help you with something?" I try to ask confidently, but it came out more meek than I intended.

He shakes off whatever strange emotion he was feeling and cracks a wicked grin. "So you must be something special to nab yourself a player like Razboinic."

The way he says it makes me feel even slimier after the India situation, but I try to keep my face neutral.

"Let me rephrase the question: Is there something useful I can help you with other than gossip? You don't exactly strike me as the gossipy type, but I guess I've been wrong before," I say with a shrug of indifference.

The laugh that breaks through his lips startles the both of us, which makes me giggle. How long has it been since someone has laughed, if it startles them when they do?

Once he's regained his composure, he extends his hand to

me in a gentlemanly way and says, "I'm Khaos. Khaos Mokotoff. I'm the team captain of the Augusta Vultures."

I extend my hand, meeting his, trying to place him.

He leans in and leaves a light kiss on the top of my hand, which feels all wrong when I realize who he is.

"You played against them the first home game!" I nearly yell, snatching my hand away from him, "You were the one that hit him!" I snarl, backing away from him. He looks far too pleased with himself that I finally recognized him.

"And you're the one that was dragged screaming from the arena. I had to meet the little woman that cared so deeply for a giant brute like him." He has an almost sleazy tone, but it doesn't feel genuine.

Again, my brain is telling me I should be afraid of him, but something inside me says otherwise. Just because I'm not afraid of him doesn't mean I'm going to hang out with someone who could hurt Roman like that.

"I think you should leave." I say, crossing my arms over my chest.

He doesn't respond, and he doesn't look like he has any plans of leaving.

Not until one of the employees comes to lead me to the locker room area. I'm thankful for the escape. I just want to see Roman. Too much has happened this evening.

It feels like forever before he comes through the locker room door, his hair still dripping water from his shower. In two giant steps, he's swooping me in a circle and into his arms. I can't help the giggle that escapes me, as I'm filled with the warmth and electricity only he can give me.

I release a deep sigh and snuggle closer as he nuzzles into

my neck and mumbles, "I'm so fucking sorry, Leera. I'm so sorry for putting you in that position."

I try to hold on to my anger, but I just can't. Not with him. "I want to be mad at you, but I can't. But I also never want to feel like that again. You have to tell her," I say, trying to reign in my emotions, "she almost made a scene. Basically, she called me the other woman in front of everyone around us. I stood up to her and got her to leave me alone this time, but I don't think I'll be as lucky next time." I finish, feeling small. Well smaller than I am.

He holds me closer and continues to apologize.

"That's not all." I say quietly.

At that, he pulls his head back to look at me and asks, "What do you mean?"

"Khaos came over to talk to me at the end of the game. He just said he wanted to meet me, and he kissed my hand. But he looked at me funny. Like I confused him."

Roman seems to think for a moment before his expression darkens with something that might be worry.

"I think . . . I think he might have felt a bond with you . . ."

"WHAT?! I don't want more than one mate!" I say a bit too loudly, forgetting we're still in a hallway in a hockey arena.

"Let's get you to the car, and I'll explain what I think it was," he says.

"Can't you just tell me what's going on now?!"

"While there are many werewolves here, there are also a lot of humans. Not to mention, if we don't get out of here soon, the press will catch up with us after our display tonight."

Crap, that makes sense. So I nod and take his hand as he ushers me through the building.

He stops in front of a shining silver Mercedes. I've never found cars to be any level of attractive, but of course this man would own a car that feels sexy.

"I don't remember seeing this one in your garage." I say, and he opens the passenger door for me to climb inside. I'm about to drop in when I see my name stitched into the seat in pink embroidery.

"It's brand new. I had it custom ordered when I couldn't get the color silver out of my mind." He's proud of himself, but he also looks worried, waiting for my response.

"Why is my name on the seat?"

"Because this is our car. No one else will ever ride there but you, sweetheart."

And dammit, if my heart doesn't melt a little more for this man.

Once I allow myself to fall into my seat, I see all the little pink features he's added, and I'm just in awe.

He rounds the car and climbs in himself, and he just looks at me for what feels like forever.

"Do I have something in my teeth?" I joke, which brings him back to reality.

"I just still can't believe you're real. I don't think I'll ever believe it," he says, shaking his head as he starts the car.

"Okay, so this weird bond?" I press, smashing the moment we were having to smithereens.

"Right, so wolves don't only have mate bonds. There are pack bonds. And there are . . . family bonds."

I scrunch my eyebrows in confusion.

"I've never met Khaos before, how can I be his family?"

Roman's head drops, nearly resting on the steering wheel.

"There's more to the rivalry between Khaos and I, than hockey." He begins, and I just wait for him to continue.

Heaving a heavy sigh, he continues. "Khaos is only a year younger than me. Our fathers put us against each other all the time. He grew up in my shadow, but I was never crude to him or anything . . . we just never could meet eye-to-eye after growing up constantly competing against each other. It ended up causing abrasion between our parents as well, and our lack of friendship grew into an angry beast," he says, shaking his head.

"Imogen was his little sister. He was blind with rage over our mate bond. He didn't want her to be sucked into the royal pieces of our world that involved me being the commander of the army. He tried to keep her from me, just as my father tried to keep me from her. Then, when she was killed, he blamed me—justifiably so. So with you being my reincarnated mate, you share the same soul as Imogen. He feels her within you. It probably scared him, like it did me. But since a family bond isn't as strong or sacred, his reaction wasn't as strong as mine."

My mind is reeling. I just got used to the idea that I might be a freaking werewolf with a seven hundred year old mate, and now I learn his seven hundred year old arch nemesis is basically my brother.

I don't even know what to say.

"Um, okay. Can we add that to our table of conversations for later? Wait, where are we going?"

"After a win, especially at home games, the boys all go out and party. I thought we could go back to my place and watch a movie or something, unless, of course, you want to go home," he asks.

"Are you sure you don't want to go to the party? I don't

want you to miss stuff just because of me. I'm just not really good with that kind of energy yet. Zoey tried taking me to one, and I had a panic attack before she could finish her first drink."

His eyes never leave the road as he caresses the side of my face, and I can't help but lean into him when he says, "Everything I need for the rest of my existence is right here."

35
ROMAN

My smart-ass little mate chose to watch Twilight again after I said she could choose anything. I should have known by the ornery twinkle in her eye. It was too similar to the twins' faces, pretty much all the time. I'll have to remember to stay alert if I ever catch the three of them potentially scheming. I have a feeling the three of them could definitely cause me some stress.

We didn't actually watch any of the movie except for when she'd stop talking to me long enough to quote her favorite parts. It was ridiculous, and adorable. The talking was everything, though. She told me about her life growing up with her parents. Regarding her parents, she's decided we're not talking about the poison right now either. I wonder if it has to do with why she's so small. There are small werewolves, but I mean, she's unusually smaller than most. I wonder if the size of her wolf was also impacted.

If we keep tabling all the weird things we learn about her, we're never going to get through it all. But she's been through so much, and I don't want to push her too hard.

She's starting to doze off now, but I can't bring myself to want to take her home.

"Leera, honey, you're falling asleep. Do you want me to take you home?" I ask softly.

"Y-you want me to leave?" she asks with the saddest, sleepiest eyes I've ever seen.

I scoop her body into my arms so fast that I worry she'll have whiplash. "No, baby, that's not it at all. I just wanted to make sure you wouldn't be uncomfortable if you woke up here in the morning."

Her head is laying over my heart, and she grips onto my shirt. "Can we have a G-rated sleepover?" she asks in her sweet, sleepy voice, causing a gravelly laugh to escape me.

"Of course we can. Would you like something comfortable to sleep in? Do you want to sleep in a guest room or . . ." I trail off, and she stills.

She slowly lifts her eyes to mine, and while she's still sleepy, there's a bit of fire in her icy eyes. "I'd love to be with you tonight if you think we can stick to a G rating. I'm not ready for . . . mph—" I stop her with my finger on her plush pink lips. I shouldn't have touched her lips. Now I know they really are as soft as they look.

Growling softly, I think I regain my composure before she notices my internal struggle: "I promised you slow, and I meant it. I would like to hold you if you're okay with that."

She gives me a small nod with a soft smile, causing a light blush to bloom all over her face.

"Do you have a spare t-shirt I could wear? Is that okay? Should I just leave all this on?"

"I would love to see you in one of my shirts," I say, trying not to growl this time. *Goddess, help me.*

Her whole body is flushed with desire now. The sight and scent nearly bring me to my knees in the middle of the hallway, but I force myself to continue. She remains oblivious to my current struggle, just holding onto me with that soft smile on her face.

I carry her upstairs and into my large bedroom. My room is fairly bare. I've never cared to decorate, but she still looks around in awe. I show her the bathroom, closet, and my dresser, giving her access to anything she needs and giving her time to get comfortable.

I sprint back down to the kitchen and splash cold water on my face. *It's going to be a LONG night.*

After about half an hour, I make my way back to my room and slowly open the door. I find her perfect little body tucked under the blanket, with her head peeking out the top and a sweet smile on her face.

I walk over to the dresser, having already changed and showered in the locker rooms. I start to raise my shirt towards my head when I hear a small, sharp intake of breath.

Smiling to myself and pretending I didn't hear her, I very slowly remove the shirt the rest of the way from my body. Once I've tossed the shirt to the side, I hook my thumbs in my joggers and slowly pull them down my body, leaving only my lounge shorts I had on underneath.

I turn around just as the scent of her desire hits me again, but it's stronger this time, like a truck, and I find her eyes blown a little with lust and realize I'm only going to end up torturing myself.

"Is this okay?" I ask, not wanting to make her uncomfortable at all, even though I can clearly see she's happy with what she sees.

Still just a small nod and an embarrassed smile.

I climb into bed next to her and pull the covers over myself, before turning to her. She's lying somewhere between her side and her back, holding the covers in front of her.

"The princesses in kids movies get a kiss goodnight." I say quietly as I push the hair from her face.

Another nod, and she starts tangling her fingers together.

"Leera, we don't have to; I was just as—" but it's her turn to stop me with her small finger pressed against my lips. The electricity shoots straight to my dick. *What was I thinking?*

"I want you to kiss me, Roman. I just wanted to remind you that I might be bad at this. I've never done anything before. Please be patient with me."

If my name on her lips wasn't already my undoing, being reminded that I will be her first and only everything nearly causes my eyes to roll to the back of my head.

I slowly reach over, gently pulling her to me. My hand covers nearly the entire left side of her face, and I brush my thumb across her bottom lip.

Her eyes flutter closed as she leans in closer.

I meet her in the middle, softly pressing my lips to hers, and I know in that moment that if something ever happens to Leera, I won't survive it. Losing my mate once was hard enough. Getting her back like this, I just know I won't survive if I lose her.

I pull back, still caressing her soft skin with my fingertips, trying to memorize how she feels.

Her eyes flutter back open, and she just looks at me for a few moments. "Does everyone's first kiss feel like fireworks?" she asks breathlessly.

"No sunshine, that's all you."

She seems to be fighting herself on something. "What if we . . . what if we tried a PG-level kiss?" she asks, blushing furiously.

Rolling my neck to keep myself and my wolf in check, "I'll give you anything you want, Leera. On this, you're the boss."

She lifts herself so she's kind of kneeling beside me; it looks like my little mate wants to take the lead.

She grabs my hands and places them on her hips and asks, "Is this ok?"

I can only nod.

"Can I . . . can I sit in your lap?"

I smile and nod again, gripping her hips and reminding myself not to hold her too roughly.

Then, as if she's trying to kill me, she slowly moves herself to straddle my lap. I have to resort to mentally reciting hockey plays to try and keep a certain part of my body, which is currently only three layers of clothing away from her core, from startling her.

Once she's wiggled around an ungodly amount and made herself comfortable, she slides her hands up my chest. She notices the trail of goosebumps she leaves, she slightly tilts her head and asks, "I give you goosebumps too?"

"You have no idea," I try not to growl, but I fail.

She leans in, and less gently, I press my lips to hers. After a moment, I run the tip of my tongue across the seam of her lips. So incredibly slowly, she opens to me, and I'm unable to capture the growl that escapes me when I finally taste her.

She even tastes like fucking honeysuckle and spun sugar.

I move my tongue slowly against hers, letting her become accustomed to the feeling.

When a low and raspy moan escapes her, it causes her eyes to fly open. I meet hers and let her feel the heat in mine, and she closes them again.

She melts into my touch as my hands match the speed of my tongue as she starts to move her own as well.

Allowing myself a few more minutes of blissful torture, I slowly pull my lips from hers. I lost control of my need for her, though, and I know she can feel that need beneath her.

The haze of lust slowly leaves her eyes, and in an instant, she's blushing harder than ever before.

"How were your first kisses, then?"

"They felt like everything was right in the world. They felt like coming home. They felt like you're going to be trouble." She giggles, but she's not wrong.

I lift her off of my lap, careful to avoid my painfully hard dick. I gently set her back on her side of the bed and pull the blanket back up as I ask, "I'd like to hold you tonight, if that's okay with you."

Blushing so hard, she looks like she has a fever. She curls into my side and lays her head on my chest. I circle my arm around her, and we only manage a couple of sentences of conversation before she's asleep.

I stare down at her in sweet serenity and brush the hair from her face, kissing her forehead.

"I will do anything it takes to bring you happiness for the rest of my existence." I promise her in the dark.

I allow myself to follow her into sleep, and for the first time in hundreds of years, I sleep peacefully.

36
India

"Hello," I answer my phone. It's after midnight, and I'm tired, but I'm still so fucking mad about that little bitch trying to steal my king.

I've always wanted Roman, but at this point, there's more than just him on the line. I will be the queen. I will have power, and not even Daddy can tell me what to do anymore.

I called Daddy earlier and told him everything. I hate how calm he is when I'm so mad, but I know he'll fix it for me.

"Hello, India. Your father called me to let me know we have a bit of a situation. He didn't give me a lot of details, though. I was hoping you could start at the beginning. Tell me everything."

Ugh, why can't people just communicate with each other? It's like having to call those stupid customer service numbers where every time you're transferred, you have to start at the beginning again.

Now I have to spend another thirty minutes telling him everything that I already told Daddy.

When I'm finished, all he says is, "I see."

"How can you both be so calm about this?! Everything we've been working for, for centuries is going to be ruined!"

"Because we already have a plan, India, and that plan requires you to be on your best behavior."

"And what is this brilliant plan of yours?" I snap.

"My sources say the girl went home with him last night. So we know where she is. She has to go home eventually."

"And what exactly am I supposed to do?"

"Have an alibi and play nice, kiss ass, whatever you have to do to keep the target off your back and ours."

"How the fuck am I supposed to do that when your son fucking hates me?!"

"You're a grown woman, India; figure it out."

He hangs up before I have a chance to ask what the fuck he thinks I've been trying to do basically my entire life.

I was born and raised with the knowledge of our father's plans to take the throne.

I grew up in the castle.

I was raised like a princess.

I will be Queen.

There is no other option.

37

Leera

The sun is peeking through the curtains that are swaying in the air, stirred by the ceiling fan. I slowly allow my eyes to open, taking in my surroundings in the light of day.

As I look around the room, hoping to learn anything I can about Roman, I notice everything is new and clean, but there doesn't seem to be any personal touches anywhere.

My watch is yelling at me for forgetting my vitamins last night, so I dismiss my missed alerts.

I have a handful of texts from Zoey too; I should have texted her not to wait up. There are things about having a roommate that I'm still quite accustomed to.

With a comfortable sigh, the night before comes flooding in. Those kisses. His body. I'm glad he's taking my wishes so seriously because it would have been way too easy to get carried away last night.

I fell asleep with my head on his chest, listening to his heart beat in rhythm with mine.

Now I'm lying on my right side, facing the window. There's

a giant arm wrapped around my middle, anchoring me to the bed.

Memories from last night continue to flow through my mind, and they set a fire low in my belly. The very first kiss rocked me to my core. I don't know what came over me; I'm going to blame my wolf for now, because I would have never taken charge like that on my own.

Did you just snort at me? I ask my wolf, trying not to giggle.

And, oh my gosh, that second kiss.

Now I know what people mean when they say things got out of control and just happened. I felt like my need for him was taking over my body. It felt so good, but it was slightly terrifying to feel that out of control in my own body.

I'm glad I talked to him ahead of time about my expectations for the evening. It really was so perfect.

"You're thinking very loudly," the large body behind me grumbles with the most gorgeous morning gravel voice I've ever heard. The movies do not get this moment right. You can't capture or recreate this. You have to live it.

"Just how perfect last night was."

His hold on me tightens, and our bodies mold together. We truly feel made for each other in this moment, and I never want to leave.

"So what's the plan for the day?" I ask.

"Let's start with breakfast. Matilda makes the best breakfast in the world," he grumbles, his face still settled in the crook of my neck.

"Breakfast sounds perfect, but I have a request first. If it's not okay, that's totally fine; I just wanted to ask." I ask bashfully.

"I told you, anything I can give you, is yours."

I wriggle out of his hold and turn to face him with my most pitiful puppy dog eyes when I ask, "Can I snuggle your wolf for a few minutes? I've only got to see him the one time, and I haven't met my wolf yet, AND last time it was ruined by she-who-won't-be-named."

He's laughing by the time I finished, but he's stepped out of bed as I try to ignore the morning tent in his shorts, causing a fresh blush to bloom across my skin. When I cross my arms and pout like a rotten toddler, he laughs again as he shifts.

I will never get used to that. I still can't believe this is real life. How will it feel to shift? It just looks so magical.

I'm swooning all over again when he approaches me and nudges my hand with his giant nose. *He's so beautiful.* I guess my wolf agrees because I think she's purring.

"Pets or scratches?" I ask, holding each hand out with each option, allowing him to select the hand to tell me what he wants. He chooses scratches and rolls over on his back like an overgrown lap dog, and it's my turn to laugh.

His creamy-colored fur is so soft. "One night, can we sleep snuggled up like this?" I ask into his fur.

He looks at me, then his body, then the bed, and seems to raise an eyebrow, causing another small fit of giggles.

"You're right, it would probably be a tight squeeze. Maybe someday, in the far off future, we could get a giant bed for wolf snuggles," I think out loud.

He shifts so fast that I nearly hit the floor where I was lying against him.

He turns away to grab a robe, but not fast enough because, *wow.* From behind, his body is just as gorgeous. He's all golden muscles and valleys, and I just want to touch all of him. Once the robe is secure, he turns to face me, and he's just staring at me.

"D-did I do something wrong?"

He wordlessly shakes his head for a moment before explaining, "You . . . you spoke about our future like it really is OUR future," and I swear his voice cracks, splintering my heart.

Are his eyes glassy?!

With a small smile and an equally small nod, "I did. It just kind of came out."

I wait for him to say something, but he's still speechless.

"I mean, sure, I'm new to all this, but . . . but I can feel it," I say, tapping my hand over my heart and taking a step towards him. "It doesn't matter that my brain says none of this is possible. My soul is telling me that you are very important to us. If we were truly made for each other, who am I to turn against my fate?" I say with a smirk and a shrug, "I just want the human version of a happily ever after too."

I'll never get used to how fast he is.

I've barely registered that he came barreling across the room and picked me up, and now I'm being spun in a circle through the room as laughter spills from my lips all on its own.

"I'll never know what I did to deserve you, but I'll spend eternity making sure you know what you mean to me and thanking the Goddess for every minute," he says as he brings my body to his with another searing kiss.

38
ROMAN

Seeing Matilda and Leera together is just the cutest thing. *Goddess, I've gone soft.* I've never called anything cute in my existence. *What is this creature doing to me?!*

Leera refused to let Matilda cook breakfast on her own. I learned that she loves to cook but hasn't done much since she lost her parents. So I sat at the bar and watched them bustle around the kitchen to make enough breakfast for everyone.

The men slowly started to trickle into the kitchen, being able to smell everything they were cooking in here.

Benny is the first one to stumble in; the twins are a couple steps behind him, still half asleep. "What's the occasion?" he asks. He grabs a slice of bacon from a platter, and Matilda swats at him for his impatience.

"Miss Tilly, let me help cook breakfast! I hope you all enjoy it." Leera beams. Slate heads directly for his seat at the corner barstool, and Andrei walks in with a sleepy smile on his face when he sees the abnormally large breakfast spread.

There's a massive pile of blueberry waffles, biscuits with

sausage gravy, scrambled eggs, sunny side up eggs, bacon, sausage, and fresh cut fruit.

By the time I get my mate back, she's so happy that it makes us all smile. Leera demanded Matilda eat breakfast with us, and we had a wonderful breakfast just talking to each other, and it all just felt right. We've lived here for so long, and it has never felt this much like a home before. All thanks to her.

As much as I would like to spend all my time with her today, she has homework, and I have practice.

She agrees to let me drive her home and take the opportunity to let her choose the music stations, so I can learn what she likes.

Turns out her taste in music is very eclectic. She likes a lot of different styles and artists. We started with 90's music, switched to some older stuff Taylor Swift did, a couple songs by the Red Hot Chili Peppers, before one Kane Brown song, and then Rob Zombie.

She apparently draws the line at jazz and doesn't care for a lot of newer music. She has her favorite music artists, and she doesn't need any more.

I may have driven around the city a few times to spend more time with her, and I'm fairly certain she noticed but didn't say anything. It's going to be too hard to watch her walk away. I'll need to remedy our living situations as soon as possible.

When I finally pull up to her dorm building, we've driven around long enough that I don't have time to walk her in. Because I'm a dumbass.

She begins gathering all her things, then leans across the center console. I greedily crash my lips into hers, wishing there was a way to tattoo the taste of her on my tongue.

She pulls away flushed, and breathless, with that faraway haze of lust, and I have to remind myself she's not ready.

"Have a great day, darlin'; text me."

She nods, climbs from the car, twirls around, and skips across the lawn to the door of her building.

I wave, watching her make it all the way inside before I leave for the arena.

39

Leera

I'm skipping down the halls of the dorm, and I don't even care what I look like right now. I can't remember ever being so happy!

The closest I can remember was when my parents were on assignment in Zimbabwe and a baby elephant was born, and the mother let us spend time with him.

I fumble with my keys and get the door unlocked. As I prance into the dorm room and drop my things on my bed, I scan the area for signs of Zoey.

I wonder where she is. She should be out of class by now. I came in so distracted, I didn't check the whiteboard we got to leave each other messages on.

That sounds so perfect!

I rush into the bathroom to pull myself together real quick. I'm still wearing his T-shirt and have no desire to take it off. I swap last night's pants for a fresh pair of leggings. I throw on my Converse, grab my backpack, and fly out the door.

I stop short, realizing I don't have my phone. So I twirl back around, scramble back into the dorm room, and hunt for my phone, but can't find it. I'll text Roman from Zoey's phone to ask him to keep an eye out for it.

I blame that kiss. Happily sighing to myself, I once again exit our room and lock the door. No one's around, so I skip back down the long hallway that leads outside. *How long has it been since I skipped?* I think to myself with a pang of nostalgia.

I've no more than shut the door and taken three steps away from the building when large hands grab me all over. There's one over my eyes, one over my mouth, and two more angry hands grab my arms and start dragging me. They're shoving me with their hands and their bodies, and I'm tripping over other people's legs. The hands on my face are gloved, and all I can smell is cheap, fake leather.

As they manhandle me, they wrench my backpack from my body, and I hear the loud thud as it's dropped to the ground. For a split second, all I can think about is my home work and my laptop being left on the ground.

How will I turn in my assignments? What if someone steals my laptop? Why is that what I'm thinking right now?!

I try to scream, but no sound escapes from the hand masking my face. I didn't see anyone around. It's Saturday, no one hangs around the commons in the afternoon.

OMG, what's happening?!

I'm being hauled away, and there's nothing I can do about it! I'm trying to fight and kick, but I'm not accomplishing anything but panic. I'm too small.

I can barely breathe with this giant hand covering my mouth, it's kind of blocking my nose, and it doesn't help that I'm starting to hyperventilate.

I think I'm crying, but I can't tell anymore.

Help! Roman! Where are you?! Anyone?!

The only answer I receive feels like my wolf snarling beneath my skin, but like before, she doesn't seem as strong when we're away from Roman.

Everything happens so fast, but somehow it feels like it happens in slow motion. I'm suddenly being thrown into a vehicle of some kind, and my knees hit the metal floor hard.

I try to scream for help, but the second I do, a damp cloth is placed over my face until the whole world fades away.

to be continued.

Acknowledgements

Holy Shit. I did it. I wrote a book.

I'm not crying, you're crying.

But seriously, this is my first book baby, so this is going to be a little long winded.

Funny story: One day I was just sitting there and thought to myself, if I ever wrote a werewolf book, I would name them Roman, Leera, Benny, and India after my husband's childhood Chows. Then I was like, man, I wish there were some werewolf hockey books out there. Y'all, that's literally how this book came to be.

Okay, now I need to spread some SERIOUS love.

First, I want to throw a shout out to my husband, Daniel, for dealing with me. I know it's not easy, but you still do it. You support every crazy thing I've ever said I wanted to do. You've always called me your diamond in the rough. I've never really felt like it, but you make me want to try.

Next, I need to thank my girls.

Di. This book would not have happened without you. I'll never forget telling you my "if I wrote a book someday, it would go like this," and that conversation turning into this book. You read every chapter while I wrote and hyped me up like you would never believe. When some of my beta readers ghosted me and I thought it meant my book was shit and I second-guessed all the work I had done, you didn't let me stay down. You never do. Thank you for always being there to pick me back up.

Steph. My little sister and lifelong best friend. Dammit, I'm crying again. I love you so much, and I'm so fucking proud of the woman you grew to be. Thank you for beta-reading, hyping, lunch dates, and being the best aunt ever. The world needs more Aunt Stephs.

I also want to shout out to some very important people who made this book come to life.

CR Jane. I picked up and read her first book, First Impressions, in December of 2022. I have read over twenty of her books since. You're my favorite author. You're my friend. YOU inspired me to write this book. If I hadn't been able to write it, I even asked if you would write the story for me so I could read it. (LOL true story). Thank you for pushing me and believing in me that I could really do this.

Demi Winters. I will forever be honored that I got to beta-read The Road of Bones and The Kingdom of Claw. When I started thinking of my beta readers, I knew I wanted to offer the same to you because I would treasure your feedback. I had NO IDEA how invaluable that feedback would become. I really liked my story when I sent it to you. Your feedback made me LOVE my story.

To my Street Team Hype Squad: I love you guys! Thank

you for taking a chance on a crazy little indie author like me and loving my characters as much as I do before you even met them! Seriously. Don't cry. Don't cry. Lisa, Mara, Meg, Jaquelyn, Casey, Genevieve, Brandi, Erin, Coco, Karina, Kat, Ashley, Danielle, Sapana, Jessica, Rose, AJ, Faye, Mari, Liz, Shana, Mandi, Karlee, yall kept me going so many days. And so many more of you!

To my editor and formatter/hardcover designer: Thank you both so much for helping make my book perfect for the public.

To my other author friends that let me bug them: Thank you Casey for beta reading my baby. Thank you Stacey for constantly checking on my and hyping me up! Thank you Brittany, K., and more, for letting me ask you all my crazy, random questions.

Last, but definitely not least, thank YOU! The reader who took a chance on me and read my first ever book. I promise there is so much more coming for this gang of weirdos. I hope you're ready for a wild ride!

About the Author

IZZY ELLIOTT

is a mom of four who lives in Southwest Missouri.
Oh, Lord, I can't do this stuffiness.

Hey Y'all!
I'm **Izzy.**

I am a mom of four who lives in Missouri; that is true, but I also work full time.

I love to spend my time reading, writing, traveling, Disney-ing, taking walks outside, and shopping. I have a serious shopping problem.

You can find me on Instagram or TikTok under IzzyElliottWrites for all updates on books and merch!